DISCARDED

vs.

Aviva

vs. the

Dybbuk

Mari Lowe

LEVINE QUERIDO

Montclair | Amsterdam | Hoboken

For Abba and Ema

יגיע כפיך כי תאכל אשריך וטוב לך

This is an Arthur A. Levine book
Published by Levine Querido

LQ
LEVINE QUERIDO

www.levinequerido.com • info@levinequerido.com
Levine Querido is distributed by Chronicle Books, LLC
Text copyright © 2022 by Mari Lowe
All rights reserved
Library of Congress Control Number: 2021943713
ISBN: 978-1-64614-125-8
Printed and bound in China

MIX
Paper from
responsible sources
FSC
www.fsc.org
FSC™ C144853

Published February 2022

First Printing

Before

WHEN I WAS NINE YEARS OLD, I slipped out of our little apartment and hid in the woods, just to see if anyone would notice I was gone. Only the dybbuk saw me leave. I didn't tell my mother, and I didn't leave a note. I still don't really understand why I did it in the first place, except that it was an idea that I wasn't able to shake for a few weeks. At first, it was only a passing thought that I shrugged off. Then, it was suddenly all I could think about.

We didn't really have a *woods* in Beacon, but we did have a ragged overgrown area with a ramshackle sign in front that said *BEACON PARK*. There were high trees and weeds taller than I was, and I ran through them, my heart racing and my fists clenched with righteous fury.

I was angry that day. I don't remember why. I know I'd had an argument with my mother, but I can't remember what it was about, and I've never been brave enough to ask Ema if she remembers. She shuts down if I push too hard, and I hate seeing her eyes close off from me when she goes to her secret place.

My secret place was the woods that day, the sunset over the weeds and the trees and my rising certainty that I'd be found. Ema was going to be *furious*, I knew it, and I was ready for a real fight—the kind I had read about in books, the kind I saw my classmates have with their parents. I imagined yelling at Ema. I imagined *being* yelled at, and it filled me with new determination.

I wanted to be yelled at. I wanted to see Ema's eyes light up, just once, even if it was with rage. So I stumbled through the weeds and hunkered down in a scratchy clearing, and I waited for Ema to come for me.

But Ema didn't come. It was the end of fall, that biting time right before winter when the weather went from breezy to frigid as day turned to night, and I had forgotten my jacket at home. I shivered in the cold, rubbing my hands together and huddling against a tree, and I finally realized there was no point to waiting out in the woods. No one was coming for me.

I wanted to go back home then—I really did, more than anything—but the messy, boring little woods I'd wandered through in the daylight had become a sprawling, twisty forest at night. I walked in one direction, then another, but I couldn't find the fence that surrounded the park.

To my eyes, every movement was a wolf or a cougar—or worse, an ax murderer just waiting for little girls to stumble into the woods with him. I was afraid to shout for help and attract something worse. Instead, I picked through the weeds, walking in circles, my fists clenching harder and harder whenever I thought about crying.

I wasn't going to *cry*. I was angry, and I was going to stay angry, and when I would finally find my way home, I was going to tell Ema exactly what I thought of her. It was just the two of us in the apartment. How could she not notice I was gone? How could she not come after me?

I was a different kind of kid back then.

Eventually, though, I saw lights shining through the night, and someone calling my name. *"Aviva!"* came the shout, and I breathed a sigh of relief. *"Aviva!"*

"I'm here!" I called back, and I wiped away the tears that had leaked on to my face and ran in the direction of the light. "I'm here!"

It wasn't Ema who found me. It was Kayla Eisenberger's mother, flashlight in hand and her face wreathed in relief. She was tall, taller than I'd remembered, and she wore a smart kind of sweater with a straight skirt, all of it somehow untouched by the brambles in the woods. She ran to me, crouching to inspect my face for any bruises, and she demanded in a sharp voice, "What were you *doing* out here? What did you think—"

"Nurit," said the woman beside her. It was Mrs. Leibowitz from the school, who I only knew from the mikvah back then. She was older, round where Mrs. Eisenberger was narrow and with stray brown and gray hairs flying out from under her hat, and her eyes were gentled by crow's feet, and a surprising warmth lingering within them. Mrs. Eisenberger frowned at her, outrage still on the tip of her tongue, but she took a breath and said, "Let's bring her back to the cars. Let the others know that she was found."

There were a few cars all parked outside of the fence, and a bunch of men and women scattered around them. Most had flashlights and were coming from the woods, same as me. People had noticed I was gone, after all, but I didn't care about any of them.

I looked around, squinting at adult face after adult face, searching only for one person.

Mrs. Eisenberger saw me looking and gave me a tight smile. "She's back at your house," she said, and my heart sank. "She called Mrs. Leibowitz when she couldn't find you, but the community patrol thought she should stay at home in case you came back." Her voice was still disapproving, but she must have seen something in my eyes because her voice softened. "No injuries?" I shook my head. I had a few scrapes, but I didn't want half the community clustered around to inspect them, to see my tearstained face or to ask me why I'd done it.

I thought that Mrs. Eisenberger might push me for an explanation or maybe even snap at me for being so stupid. But instead, she inhaled, a long and tired breath, and then she put a hand on my shoulder. "Come on. I'll take you home."

Kayla was sitting in the back seat of the Eisenberger van when her mother opened the door, hands pressed to the window as she squinted out at the dim light and people flooding the area. She turned around when the car door slid open, her green-brown eyes wide as she caught sight of me, and then she looked away, twisting a lock of amber-red hair around her finger. "I guess you found her," she said, her voice flat.

Mrs. Eisenberger's phone rang. "Just a minute," Mrs. Eisenberger said, distracted, and she took out her phone and stepped away from the car. "Avishai? We'll be there soon." Avishai. That was Kayla's father.

I sat as far away from Kayla as I could, squirming against the closed door, and Kayla said abruptly, "Where were you?"

I shrugged. "I went out to the woods." I tried to sound strong and confident, like I'd imagined myself being when I'd went out to the woods in the first place, but instead, I just sounded small. Kayla glanced at me and pressed her lips together, her feet tapping against the back of the driver's seat, and she said, "I didn't come to look for you, you know. I was going somewhere with my mother."

"Where?" I said, and then I remembered that Kayla and I weren't friends anymore. I didn't know why she was talking to me in the first place, though the part of me that wasn't dull with anger was suddenly very curious.

Kayla took a breath, and she looked at me for a moment like she wanted to say something else. In that instant, I wanted to hear whatever it was that she wasn't explaining. But she didn't even answer my question. "None of your business," she said abruptly, and she kicked the back of the seat again and stared straight ahead until Mrs. Eisenberger returned to the car.

And I got my answer then, though I didn't know why it had been a secret in the first place. "Abba is waiting for us," Mrs. Eisenberger said as she started the car, and she sounded tired but happy. "He's ready to go."

Kayla only nodded, avoiding my eyes.

No one spoke for the whole drive back. Kayla glanced at me a few times, but she looked away quickly whenever I caught her staring. She opened her mouth once, as though she were about to speak, but then she snapped it shut again. I kept my eyes trained on the ripped gray vinyl of the seat in front of me most of the time. I didn't want to talk to Kayla. I wanted to hold on to my anger until I got home.

When we got to my shabby little apartment next to the shul, Mrs. Eisenberger walked me to the door, her keen eyes fixed on me as though I might run away again. I didn't know what she knew about why I'd gone missing, but I was afraid to ask. Instead, I pushed the door open and said quickly, "You don't need to come in."

I shut the door before she could follow me, and I stalked into the mikvah waiting room. It was bigger than any of the rooms upstairs in our cramped living space, darkly carpeted with a couch against the entry wall and chairs dotted around the clear-bottomed coffee table opposite it. The lights were on, and the dybbuk was watching me with solemn eyes. He was hovering over the peeling wood-brown desk that Abba had gotten from his grandfather when he'd married Ema and moved out to Beacon. I didn't see Ema anywhere.

The lights were off upstairs in the apartment, but I could hear Ema's cell phone ringing. I clenched my fists and started upstairs, ready for a fight.

The phone kept ringing. I saw it on the kitchen table when I made it upstairs, the only light glowing in the dark apartment. I snatched it up. "Hello?"

It was Mrs. Leibowitz. "Aviva," she said, and her kind voice sounded relieved. "I haven't been able to get a hold of your mother."

"She's here," I said automatically, glancing around the room. I saw Ema at last—not in the kitchen but sitting on my bed, silhouetted in the window that overlooked the front of the building. "We're fine. Thank you."

"Aviva—" Mrs. Leibowitz began, but I hung up. My rage was boiling over then, desperate for an escape. I was *so* angry, and it wasn't about the argument we'd had earlier that day. I was lost in the woods, and Ema hadn't come for me. I was *missing*, and Ema hadn't cared enough to—

I stalked through the kitchen to my room, ready for the fight I'd been itching for all day, and I said, my voice too loud in our silent apartment, "Did you even notice I was gone?"

Ema didn't respond. I took another step toward her. For a moment, I thought she was dead, that she was sitting still for so long she just froze that way. But she was breathing, light and barely audible, and I marched around to face her.

I recoiled. Ema's face was almost white, her eyes blank, and she looked right through me as though she couldn't see me. I wanted to rage at her, to let out all my frustrations and my nine-year-old fury, but it seemed like my words would only pass through her, would make her fade away more and more until I'd be shouting through air.

I must have aged a few years in those seconds alone, staring at Ema and trying to find words that wouldn't come. My anger was gone, replaced with fear and bitter regret. I shouldn't have run away, I knew. It wouldn't change anything. Nothing was going to change for us.

Finally, I said the only thing I could. "Ema," I whispered. "Isn't someone coming to the mikvah tonight?"

Ema jolted. "Aviva," she said, her voice raspy and raw. She lifted a hand to my cheek, her fingers brushing against my dried tears, and I wanted to cry again. Ema said my name with such tenderness that—for the first time all night—I wondered how I ever could have doubted her love for me.

I looked away from her, watching the lawn through the window. Behind me, I heard the bed creak as my mother got up, and a light flicked on in the kitchen. Within a few minutes, Ema was downstairs at the mikvah, and I was alone again.

I sat at the top of the stairs as I listened to a knock at the door, to Ema's low voice as she ushered the mikvah visitor in. I didn't want to see who it was or to help Ema today. I wanted to crumple under my blanket and cry for hours.

Instead, I waited until the dybbuk came to sit beside me. He smiled at me, an impish look that showed no sign of reproach or disappointment, and I exhaled and reached for him. I couldn't touch him, of course, but my hand settled just over where his hand would have been, and I kept it there and didn't cry.

The apartment was fully heated, but I was colder at that moment than I'd been in the woods, surrounded by weeds and trees and my own fury.

Chapter 1

"Kosher!" Ema's voice rings out through the room, and I poke my head against the closed door of the spare bathroom, trying to peek through to see what's happening in the mikvah. Mrs. Blumstein is in there with Ema, and I can hear a splash and then another "Kosher!"

I can't see, of course, and I know I'm not allowed to open the door, so I don't. "Kosher!" Ema calls for the third time, and I bite my lip and realize, suddenly, that the dybbuk has gotten into Mrs. Blumstein's room.

I hear more splashing and then low murmurs as Mrs. Blumstein and Ema talk. "Do you have Shabbos meals this week?" Mrs. Blumstein wants to know.

I hurry out of the spare bathroom and seize a wire hanger from the laundry room, jamming it into the lock of the main bathroom. Ema is talking, her voice muffled through the wall. "We're all set for Shabbos," she says, and I can imagine the pained smile on her face. She always gets that smile when she thinks people are trying to offer us charity. "I think we'll stay in this week."

The lock pops open. I dash into Mrs. Blumstein's room, peering around.

It doesn't take long to see what the dybbuk has done. Mrs. Blumstein's purse has been opened, and there are little candies strewn across the floor. They're all open, the wrappers lying beside them, and I hiss, "Dybbuk, *why?*" as I stare at them in consternation.

Mrs. Blumstein is chatting with Ema again. "You know, I have an eleven-year-old niece," she says, and I make a face. I know Shira Blumstein—she of the weirdly pinched nose that makes her always look like she's annoyed, who is in my class in school and doesn't talk to me. Kind of like . . . everyone in my class. Mrs. Blumstein has the same pinched nose, and when she's wearing a snug blue beanie to cover her hair, her whole face slopes back alarmingly. Somehow, it suits her like it doesn't Shira. "She'll be over at my house this weekend. Maybe we can arrange a playdate with your daughter."

Talk more, I plead frantically, glaring at the dybbuk. He's lurking against the rough, pale wall of the hallway, grinning at me with that smile he gets when he knows he's done something particularly naughty. *Typical.* I drop to the floor, picking up the candies and wrapping them as neatly as I can.

To my relief, Ema responds. "You'll have to convince Aviva, not me," she says wryly. "You know that Aviva can be . . . a little much for the other girls." I take that as a compliment. The dybbuk makes a face, and I don't waste any more time glowering at him. I have too many candies to wrap.

"Oh, Shira loves her, though," Mrs. Blumstein says, which is a *lie.* Shira is Kayla's best friend, and Kayla is never quiet about how much she hates me. "She's always talking about Aviva. Why don't you send Aviva over in the afternoon?"

Ema says, "I'll try," but there's finality in her voice, the conversation over. I panic, staring in alarm at the wrappers and candy still left on the floor, and I seize them all as the door begins to open and throw them into the toilet. I flush the toilet, the sound too loud, and Ema says suddenly, "Though, speaking of Shabbos, I have been meaning to ask you about your spinach gefilte fish."

"Oh?" Mrs. Blumstein is distracted again, and she begins to rattle off a recipe as Ema makes interested humming noises. I scramble out of the room, shoving right past the dybbuk, and clamber onto one of the ugly flowered chairs in the waiting room.

The dybbuk perches beside me on the next chair, a lazy finger hovering over the fabric of the seat. He doesn't go into the rooms when the women are inside, of course. He's a boy, if dybbuks can be boys at all. I pull a book off the coffee table and read in silence, pretending to be absorbed in it.

Ema emerges from the mikvah a few minutes later. With Mrs. Blumstein back in her room, Ema's movements are slower, and she sits heavily behind the desk before frowning at me. "What were you doing in Mrs. Blumstein's room?" she asks.

"It was the dybbuk," I say helplessly, gesturing to him. "He unwrapped all of Mrs. Blumstein's candies. I had to fix it."

Ema sighs, but she doesn't say anything more. She knows the dybbuk can't be stopped.

No one can stop the dybbuk. He's been haunting the mikvah for years, and I'm the only one who can keep track of him. Maybe it's because I grew up with him, or maybe it's because I have a little bit of Abba's magic in me. Abba used to tell stories about dybbuks and gilgulim, their souls lingering in this world or reborn into a new life. He'd share the legend of the Golem of Prague, brought to life from river clay to lumber around and defend the Jews of the city and the stories of the sheidim who would test King Solomon. I don't remember Abba very well anymore—Ema doesn't like to keep his picture around, and it's been five years since the accident— but I still remember his stories.

We'd sit together in the big chair in our old apartment, and he'd tell me all about them. "Do you know the story of the gilgul of Shalom the shammas?" he'd ask me, and I'd bounce on his lap and demand to hear it. "Shalom the shammas's job was to look after the shul and all its holy books—"

"Like you do!" I'd say every time.

"Exactly," Abba would say. "And one day, there was a great storm and Shalom the shammas was swept out to sea. No one ever saw him again." He would sound grave, and I would laugh because the idea of losing someone forever still seemed impossible to me.

Abba would brighten. "But something happened to brave little Yerachmiel, the rabbi's son. He was a little boy just about your age. For years, he had helped Shalom the shammas put away all the siddurim after davening, even when all of his friends would run off to eat at the kiddush first. He mourned Shalom the most of anyone in the town."

Abba would lean forward, his voice rising and falling, and I would snuggle in close, enchanted by the story. "One day, Yerachmiel was out near the sea when a group of Cossacks came up to him and began to yell at him, shouting insults and waving sticks and heavy clubs at him. Yerachmiel was alone, and he couldn't run away. They got closer and closer, when *suddenly*—"

And I would bounce, knowing exactly what happened next. "A crocodile!" I would shout.

"A crocodile emerged from the sea," Abba would proclaim. "Little Yerachmiel froze up, but the crocodile didn't notice him at all. Now, this was in Ukraine in the 1800s, far from any crocodile habitats or zoos. No one in that town had ever seen a crocodile before. But there was a crocodile!" He'd snap his jaws hard, and I would jump, giggling. "The men ran, and Yerachmiel was saved. And then, the crocodile walked beside him all the way back to the shul, where it lay down in front of Shalom's old seat and died."

I always thought that was a terrible waste. I would imagine Yerachmiel with a pet crocodile, scaring off anyone who might want to hurt him. He would have been the coolest kid in school for sure. But Abba was adamant that this is how the story had to go. "A gilgul exists because someone was short on good deeds in their first life. Now, a dybbuk is a different story."

He would sit back in the chair, holding out his arm so I could duck under it again, and he would say, "A dybbuk is a soul that won't rest. It didn't finish what it was supposed to do in this life, and it will create mischief right up until its mission is fulfilled."

I had never seen a dybbuk back then, but I imagined that every little creature might be a gilgul, might be another soul returned to this world to do good deeds. "Good luck," I'd whisper to ants, creeping along in our apartment. "Thank you," I'd say to the roadkill in the street. One could never be too careful.

Abba didn't come back as a gilgul. I think it's because he did lots of good deeds. Still, it's kind of sad. He would have enjoyed our dybbuk.

··

The dybbuk came with the mikvah. After the accident, we moved into a little house on top of the mikvah and Ema took over as the mikvah lady in Beacon. Beacon is small, but we're a *growing Jewish neighborhood*, whatever that means. Right over in New Beacon is a bigger, fancier mikvah, with two separate baths and ten bathrooms for women to use at the same time, and most people in Beacon use that mikvah instead.

But we still have our regulars who come once a month without fail to use the Beacon mikvah. There's Mrs. Blumstein with the pinched nose who always brings me a treat when she comes by. Mrs. Reisman's husband works nights, so she brings along her little son to run around in the waiting room with me while she's in the mikvah and freshly makes up her pretty face on her way out. There's Mrs. Feigenbaum, who is *super* old and definitely too old for the mikvah. ("It isn't our business," Ema says. "Our job is just to get the mikvah ready for anyone who needs it.")

There's Mrs. Cohn, Mrs. Kohn, and Mrs. Cohen, one tall, one short, and one in-between, like the three bears from Goldilocks. My favorite monthly visitor is Mrs. Leibowitz, who comes each time with a new book for me to read. Mrs. Leibowitz is the history teacher at my school, and she lets me sit in her office during lunch sometimes while she grades papers, losing pens under her desk and banging her head against it when she tries to get them. I don't really like to sit with my classmates.

We usually get three or four women a week. New Beacon gets loads more, maybe even twenty or thirty women a *night*. But our mikvah is just a few little rooms off of the side of the shul, and only Ema is in charge of it.

The mikvah is divided into five rooms. The biggest is the waiting room, where there is the couch and those ugly flowered chairs, along with a bunch of oversized, velvety chairs against the walls and Abba's desk and the coffee table where I like to do my homework. There are two bathrooms off the sides of the waiting room, a laundry room near the entrance, and a fourth door leading to the mikvah itself. Each bathroom has a second door, so women can go straight from the bathroom to the mikvah.

The mikvah is just a little pool, barely ten feet long and maybe five feet wide. It's deep enough that even tall Mrs. Cohn could probably duck down and be totally covered. There is another mikvah for the men on the other side of the shul, but Ema isn't in charge of that one, except to wash the linens. In front of that mikvah is an outdoor one, a third mikvah just for immersing dishes and silverware to make them kosher.

Dipping in the mikvah is supposed to make you *kosher*, pure in a way that nothing else can. One time when I was six, after we had moved into the apartment over the mikvah, I went into the mikvah and got undressed. I walked down the steps until the water was higher than my head and coughed from the chlorine. I didn't feel any holier after that, only wet. Maybe it's because I was too afraid to say the blessing while I was inside. I just wanted to go in deeper, until everything was blue and I wouldn't feel anything at all.

That's when I first met the dybbuk. I tripped on the last step and fell into the water, and everything went fuzzy all at once. I was sputtering water and scared and lost, when a hand seized mine and pulled me back toward the steps until I was able to climb back up.

I saw him then as a laughing figure, a boy as old as my cousin Ari, and then he threw my clothes into the mikvah and careened from the room.

The next time I saw him, he was pulling all the tissues out of a tissue box in the main bathroom. Then he unscrewed the hinges from the bottom of the door of the spare bathroom, *then* he put something in the laundry that turned all the towels purplish-gray, *then* he tore up a fifty-dollar check Ema had gotten from Mrs. Blumstein as a tip. That was the worst one, and Ema was really mad until I explained to her all about the dybbuk.

The dybbuk loves chaos and destruction, and he haunts our mikvah to spread it. He's the *worst*, and I spend all my time chasing him, trying to undo his messes. I'm good at figuring out what he's done right after he does it. I'm also the only one who can see him. Everyone else just sees the damage he does.

Chapter 2

I'M ELEVEN YEARS OLD, JUST TWO months away from my twelfth birthday and my Bas Mitzvah. I have frizzy brown hair that never sits neatly on my head, even when I try to pull it back, and I'm in sixth grade in school. Before the accident, I guess I had a lot of friends. Ema was the most popular teacher in the eighth grade, and my whole class used to run to her when we saw her in the hall. Kayla and I were best friends and next-door neighbors.

After the accident, things changed. *Ema* changed. I don't remember much of how she was around Abba back then, but I remember how she used to laugh. Now, she's quiet, and she doesn't go out to visit friends anymore. They used to come over at first, to visit and to invite us for the big Shabbos meals our community has every Saturday, that are full of steaming hot potato kugel and breaded schnitzel and challah with a shiny egg glaze, soft in the middle. Those meals always come with *people*, loads of company and the sound of a dozen guests singing the same Hebrew songs in slightly off-key melody. Ema would accept their invitations and then find a reason to cancel at the last minute on Friday, and eventually, her old friends got the message.

Her old friends were my friends' mothers, and when they stopped coming, so did their daughters. We moved away from our bright street with wide sidewalks and flat double driveways long enough to play machanayim, the rows and rows of three-family paneled houses and the crowd of children who lived in it, and we moved into the three-room apartment on top of the mikvah. Ema doesn't go outside now, except to get the linens from the other mikvah and to tidy up. Every week, the ladies who come to the mikvah invite us for the Shabbos, and every week, we stay in our quiet little apartment.

That suits me just fine. I don't need company or friends. I have Ema, Ema has me, and that's enough.

"Aviva!" barks a sharp voice, jerking me from my thoughts. Morah Miller is frowning at me under her round glasses, and I realize sheepishly that I've been tapping my feet against the floor, thumping my desk back and forth. "*Sheket bevakasha*," Morah Miller says reprovingly, and I quiet down obediently.

We are studying Hebrew grammar in class, and I can already tell that it, along with most of school, is not going to be my thing. Kayla's hand is up every time Morah Miller begins a question, smug with her knowledge, and I click my pen absently, listening to Morah Miller's sigh. "Does anyone *else* know the answer?" she says, and Kayla grins, white teeth flashing under her freckled cheeks. The class giggles.

Quiet Hodaya raises her hand and offers an answer, and Morah Miller goes on. I click my pen some more, glancing wistfully out the window of Beacon Torah Day School. It's a gorgeous day outside, the kind where it should be illegal to make kids sit inside all day. The sky is clear, and I can see planes taking off and landing at the nearby airport from the window. A seagull flaps past, twisting around abruptly, and—

"I'm *trying* to think," Shira's voice rings out, "but I can't when Aviva keeps clicking that pen!" I blink, twisting around to see all eyes on me again. Shira's pinched nose is all scrunched up, of course, and a few girls shift uncomfortably and avoid my gaze.

Morah Miller sighs. "Aviva," she says, not unkindly. "Why don't you go for a walk?"

There's a low laugh in the classroom again, this time tinged with a little more unkindness. I get asked to *go for a walk* a lot during Morah Miller's class. My other teachers are a little less tolerant. Mrs. Schwartz just sends me out of the room during science, and Ms. Horowitz makes me move my desk right against the wall.

The walks are the best. I head out of the classroom, wandering down the hall toward the door to the roof. Officially, students aren't allowed on the roof without supervision, but it's close enough to recess that I can get away with it.

I'm nearly at the door when it opens, and Mrs. Leibowitz emerges, wearing a sheitel for school that still can't conceal those flyaway graying hairs at her temples. She catches sight of me, and her eyes light up, a rosy tint to her cheeks at the chill on the roof. "Aviva," she says, drawing out my name into a melodic A-*vee*-va that sounds less exasperated than she looks. "I *know* you have Hebrew class right now."

I shrug, sheepish. "Morah Miller sent me on a walk," I admit, making a face. "She didn't say it should be *inside*."

Another teacher might have scolded me. Mrs. Leibowitz laughs, the wind swallowing up the end of it. "Aviva, Aviva," she says, shaking her head. "What are we going to do with you?"

I look up at her through my eyelashes, puppy-dog pout firmly in place. Mrs. Leibowitz gives me a look that says she knows exactly what I'm doing, but she sighs. "Two minutes," she offers, pushing open the door that leads to the roof. "Then back to class."

We walk upstairs together, and Mrs. Leibowitz says casually, "Do you have Shabbos plans already, or would you and your mother like to come over to my house Friday night for the meal?"

She hasn't been at the mikvah this week, so there's been no opportunity for a polite brush-off. I walk warily beside her, stepping out on to the roof and turning to walk its perimeter. "We're all set for Shabbos," I echo Ema. "Plus, it'd be weird to go to your house. You're my *teacher.*"

Mrs. Leibowitz studies me for a moment, and I squirm, self-conscious. It's not like I don't *like* Mrs. Leibowitz. Ema likes her too. But it's just not what we do. I speed up my pace, and she keeps up, walking beside me with a long-legged stride. "Well, if you ever decide it isn't weird . . ." she says, but she doesn't push anymore.

We walk in comfortable silence around the roof, and Mrs. Leibowitz ventures, "How about coming over when I'm not there? I have a wedding next Monday night, and I've been looking for a babysitter. My older girls *insist* they're too busy with midterms to do anything but study." She looks at me, hopeful again. "I think you'd be great with my little ones. *And* they go to sleep early, so it'd mostly be a few hours of sitting in my living room doing nothing."

I consider that. I've never babysat before, not beyond Mrs. Reisman's son at the mikvah, but we could always use the money. Ema manages with what her mikvah job pays her, and we have enough money for food and sometimes new clothes for me when I have a growth spurt.

But lately, my socks have been threadbare, and one of my expensive uniform skirts has torn at the waist. I pinned it, and I haven't told Ema about it yet. The last time I ripped a skirt we weren't able to afford, Ema sank onto the couch and sat there, eyes blank, for a long time. I crouched in a corner with the dybbuk, watching her, my fingernails digging into my palm.

If I babysit for a few hours, I can pay for the skirt myself. "I can do that," I say. "I just have to check with my mother."

"Of course," Mrs. Leibowitz says hastily, but she's smiling broadly. "Great. That's great. Now . . ." She makes a show of looking down at her watch, and she pats me on the back. "Your two minutes are up. *Scram.*" I take off, and Mrs. Leibowitz laughs behind me, the dark brown hair of her usually neat sheitel whipping in the wind.

I feel pretty windswept too, and I must look it because Morah Miller looks dubiously at me as I shove the door open and fly back into my seat. It's easier to sit for the rest of class, though, and I can focus on what she's saying as she wraps up the lesson. I'm not *stupid*, no matter what Kayla says about me. I pick up what she's been saying all day about masculine and feminine nouns in the last five minutes of class. I'll figure out the rest of it later.

My attention is beginning to wander again by the time Morah Miller, her sweet voice rising like a bell chime, calls me to attention: "Before I let you out for recess, I have a few announcements."

I perk up. *Announcements* can mean an upcoming test, or they can mean a surprise assembly downstairs in the auditorium and something good. Kayla whispers something to Shira, and they lean forward, excited. Morah Miller smiles. "As you know, the school is arranging an outing in a few weeks to celebrate your Bas Mitzvahs," she says.

I bite my lip. Every one of us will become Bas Mitzvah when we turn twelve. It's a pretty big deal, an event to mark our maturity and us becoming women, real members of the Jewish people. Some of my classmates already had their Bas Mitzvah parties with dancing and food in big halls, and the school likes to do something too. I know about the outing. It's the highlight of the year, a father-daughter party where the school rents out the Beacon Arcade, with games and competitions and pizza and ice cream. Abba would probably have loved it.

I can feel eyes flickering toward me, and I stare at my desk, clicking my pen again. Morah Miller clears her throat. "As your Bas Mitzvah is all about celebrating your entry into womanhood," she says, "this year, we're happy to announce a mother-daughter event at the Beacon Arcade with live music, dancing, and everything else you've come to expect from the Beacon Bas Mitzvah Bash." She beams at the class, careful not to look at me.

I sit in startled silence, my thumb pressing against the cap of the pen until it's sore. I can hear the murmurs of my classmates, the whispers and the stares. *Mother-daughter.* This has *always* been an event for fathers and daughters, and there's no doubt in my mind exactly why the school changed it this year.

"Why?" Shira bursts out. "Why not—My father's been talking about it for months!" She looks outraged. "We have loads of mother-daughter events. Can't we just have this one thing the way that everyone else does?"

I flush, slouching in my seat, feeling unfriendly eyes on mine. "We *just* had a mother-daughter brunch last month," another girl says, toying with the giant purple bow of her headband. "My sisters got to do the Bas Mitzvah Bash with my father. It's not fair."

It's not fair! The fury rises to a crescendo in the class, and I want to cry, to say it's *fine*, to say that my mother isn't going to go anyway. Ema doesn't go to any of the school's special events or my class plays or *anything*, really. And this might be the big one, but it's still not enough to—

But I don't say anything. Morah Miller is patiently answering questions, careful not to glance at me once. The other girls are protesting hotly, disappointed at the change in the program, but Morah Miller is immovable. "You are having the exact same event. We couldn't have live music with your fathers around, and we couldn't have dancing. The school is trying to make this event better for all of you," she says. "Nothing is changing."

Kayla glares at Morah Miller, her eyes narrowed and hard. "We want the same one as everyone else," she says loudly, and the rest of the class chimes in again. "We want our fathers there!" She tosses me a resentful look, and she mutters, "If you want us all to bring someone, then let Aviva bring her dybbuk."

Kayla doesn't say it quietly enough, and more than a few people sitting between us hear her. My face burns with hurt and shame. There's a ripple of almost embarrassed laughter through the class, a few furtive glances at me from those who don't laugh, and I lose my temper. It has been too many years since I let myself care about what Kayla Eisenberger has to say, and I won't start caring now. "Maybe I will," I snap. "Maybe he'll take care of *you*."

Kayla tosses her burnt-orange hair where it's tied back with a scrunchie, face stubborn under her freckles, and I regret ever telling my classmates about the dybbuk. I was younger when I told them. Dumber, too, to actually think it might make me friends, might make people stop treating me like an outcast.

"Aviva," Morah Miller says warningly. She gives Kayla a sharp look as well, and I slouch in my seat and imagine what the dybbuk might do to Kayla at Beacon Arcade. Break the game she's playing, maybe. Trip her while she's dancing. Wrap her up like a mummy in a long string of tickets and let her topple to the floor while everyone laughs at her instead of me.

I'm so absorbed in my vengeful daydreaming that I almost miss it when Morah Miller says, "And one more thing that I know will have you all excited." She's smiling again, happy to share this news. "The Beacon TDS machanayim team has four empty slots this year for sixth grade alternates."

She clears her throat over a new, excited murmur that ripples through the classroom. "*Please* try to remember that we have sixty-three girls in the sixth grade, which means that even some of our top players aren't going to make it. The seventh grade has eight slots on the team, and the eighth grade has ten. You'll get your chance next year if you don't get it this year."

No one is listening to her plea. Kayla is beaming, her irritation with me forgotten, and Esther and Avital are cheering in the back of the room. Morah Miller sighs, smiling at us wryly. "Tryouts will be this Thursday at lunch," she says, conceding to the mood of the room. "*Hatzlacha!*"

She said good luck to everyone, but Morah Miller's eyes flicker toward me for a moment. I sit up, my pen falling from my grip, and I grin.

Machanayim. It's kind of my thing.

Chapter 3

MACHANAYIM IS SORT OF LIKE DODGEBALL, if dodgeball had four sections. The middle two sections have the same idea—members of each team hurl a ball at someone on the other team, and if they're hit with a live ball, then they're out, but not really out.

In machanayim, you're never really out. There's another section behind the enemy team, where the captain of your team is waiting, and each person who gets out goes to join the captain there. The enemy team is surrounded on both sides, and so are you.

We play machanayim at recess, and it's the only time of day when my classmates aren't fed up with me. Instead, they're all yelling my name. "Aviva!" The ball is thrown to me, and I swing around just in time, catching it and throwing it directly at Elisheva Mozarowsky. She dodges, long ponytail flying through the air, but I'm too fast, and the ball nicks her and bounces to the ground before Kayla picks it up.

When the ball hits the ground, it's dead and can't get anyone out. Kayla is *really* good though, maybe as good as I am. She hurls the ball high, too high for any of us to catch it, and it comes down just in time for a flash of the blue and gray of our uniform as Shira snags it out of the air.

Shira is the other team's captain today. We're all energized at the idea of being a part of the school machanayim game. Every year, Beacon TDS plays a game against the Hebrew Academy of River's Edge, and most years, HARE totally crushes us. We're good, but they're *unreal*. We last won eight years ago, back when Morah Miller was in the eighth grade here.

Sixth graders are only allowed to be alternates, backup players in case the seventh- and eighth-grade players aren't there that day or have to step out. But even being an alternate means you're basically guaranteed a position next year, and it's still more than most people will get.

I have it in the bag. Shira throws the ball at me, and I snatch it out of the air, whirling around and flinging it back at Kayla. It's a risky move. If Kayla catches it, then she'll have a live ball, and she's the only one on her team who's a match for me.

She catches it against her abdomen, lurching back and then bouncing forward to slam it into tiny Hodaya's side. It bounces toward me and I throw it up, over Kayla's team to Esther Klein on my team's other side.

Esther throws it at Shayna, who dodges it and lets it roll on to my side. Esther and I volley the ball, her uniform polo flying up to reveal a brightly colored undershirt as she tosses it to me, and it's back in my hands and alive a few moments later.

I get another girl out before Kayla has the ball again, cleanly working with Shira to knock out two of my teammates. We're down to three people still in, and I smile.

I'm not always the best team player. Sometimes, I have to be reminded to let others get the ball or to pass it. But it's only because when I'm on the machanayim court, I forget sometimes that I'm playing at all. When the crowd of girls is down to just a few, I feel like I'm dancing, like the entire world around me is just a ball and fuzzy targets ahead. I whirl in circles, taunting my opponents by hovering in front of them and then dodging away.

Sometimes I like to imagine I'm a dybbuk, careening through the court like my dybbuk flies through the rooms of the mikvah. I can create chaos too, can throw the ball to the other side and watch girl after girl retreat.

And on the machanayim court, I'm actually *someone*. I can hear people shouting my name—"Aviva! Aviva! Over here!" It feels good, being good at something. Being known for something. When I focus for a moment, eyes flickering outside of the court, I see Ahuva Rennert, the eighth-grade captain of the Beacon TDS machanayim team, standing on the side and watching me with interest.

And when I look back at the other team, I see Kayla zooming across the court, ready to intercept the ball I throw at her teammate. She sends it flying back at me like a cannonball, and I catch it with an "oof!" as all the air is pushed from my stomach. Kayla's eyes are narrowed, and I can see the resentment in them as I fling the ball back at her.

We still have a few teammates each, but we've forgotten them in favor of throwing the ball at each other. Kayla smashes the ball at my side, and I dip back just enough to catch it, sending it crashing into her legs. She manages to grab it, hurling it at me again, and there is no more exhilaration in this. This isn't fun, this is angry, and there are a few voices calling Kayla's name now, cheering for her.

Kayla used to be my best friend, once upon a time. Now she has her entire team shouting for her, rooting for her to take me down. She's glaring at me as though all of this is my fault—as though the school's decision to swap out the usual Bas Mitzvah Bash is *my* fault, as though I've ruined everything just by existing—and it makes me mad too.

Catch this, I think, firing the ball at her with a little more energy than absolutely necessary. It's high, high enough that she has to jump a little to catch it at her shoulder. She throws it back before she lands on the ground, raising it and smashing it toward my feet.

I drop, catching it cleanly, and Kayla sneers at me. The girls are shouting, "Kayla! Kayla!" and I can barely hear my team with the horde of cheers behind me. I see red, and I throw the ball with extra force, as hard as I can possibly manage, directly at Kayla's face.

Kayla's eyes grow wide and alarmed. She dodges the ball instead of catching it, and I register relief in that instant instead. I didn't *mean* to throw it so hard—

The ball flies past Kayla to the teammate half-dozing behind her, smashing into poor Rikki Feldman's pale, pretty, porcelain-perfect face.

▪▪▪

They think Rikki has a broken nose. By the time the nurse arrived upstairs, Rikki's face looked oddly misshapen and swollen, purpled from the force of the ball. Kayla and I stood to the side as the others crowded around Rikki, giving us dark looks.

"This is your fault," I mutter to Kayla as we sit outside the principal's office, waiting to be called in. The teacher on roof duty is conferring with Principal Axelrod now, the two of them looking very grave through the door window. "Why didn't you catch the ball?"

"Because you were trying to *kill* me," Kayla hisses. "You ruin everything!"

"You ruined it first!" I shoot back. I don't know what I've *done* to earn Kayla's hatred. I just know she hates me, that she's hated me since second grade when everything went wrong. "I didn't *do* anything."

"You threw the ball," Kayla says hotly. "You annoy everyone in school. And now you've ruined the Bas Mitzvah Bash." She scowls at me, her pale face flushed with anger. "Couldn't you have just stayed home from that, like you always do?".

I refuse to respond, glowering at nothing at all. The secretary gives us both a concerned look, as though she thinks we might break into a fistfight right now. Instead, Principal Axelrod's office door opens and she calls out, "Aviva? Kayla?"

I drag my feet as I stand. Kayla marches into the office ahead of me, her fists clenched like she's ready to fight. "Aviva started it," she says. "Aviva hurt Rikki. I don't know why I'm here—"

Principal Axelrod puts up a hand. Kayla falls silent. Principal Axelrod has that effect on everyone. She's a little old lady, old enough that she became a great-grandmother a few years ago. Her office always smells like the perfume she uses, sweet without being overpowering. Most of the time, she's cheerful and warm, hiding treats in her office for girls who get sent there a little too often. (That's me.) I hate disappointing her, and I scuff my feet against the carpet and sit when Principal Axelrod motions.

"You were playing a game," she says. "A game in which a girl got hurt. Morah Sasson says that you two might have gotten . . . a little heated." She says it delicately, as though she knows it was a lot worse than that. "Aviva," she says, and she looks at me with a sigh. "Kayla." Now it's Kayla who shuffles, staring at the ground. "What's going on with the two of you? I remember when you two were good friends, back when you started here."

Back when we started here was in the first grade and the beginning of second grade, when I stayed home from school for a long time after the accident. Kayla stopped visiting eventually. I remember her coming over with her mother once or twice, shifting from foot to foot and starting up conversations, but I can't remember what I said in response. When I came back to school, she kept her distance, so I did too.

Kayla mutters, "That was a long time ago." She doesn't look at me. I watch Principal Axelrod instead of Kayla, my feet tapping restlessly against the carpet as the principal rubs the pendant of her necklace thoughtfully.

She studies us for a long time. Finally, she says, "I see no choice but to ban you both from the machanayim team this year."

"No!" For once, we speak in unison, allied in our horror. "We're the best—"

"It was an accident! I'll be more careful—"

"I didn't *do* anything! You can't—"

"I certainly can," Principal Axelrod says, her voice ringing out over ours. "And I am very concerned over the kind of anger that has the two of you trying to *hurt* each other in my school." She doesn't look quite so kindly anymore. Now, she's authoritative, looking down at both of us with steely eyes. "I think some time together might do you two good." She considers, then nods in sudden satisfaction. "I'm sure you two have already heard about the plans for a new Bas Mitzvah Bash," she says.

Kayla sulks. I chew on my lip. Principal Axelrod sighs. "I'm already seeing some pushback from the girls," she says, as though we're fellow teachers rather than two of said girls. "But we've been talking about changing this event for years now."

"It was fine the way it was," Kayla mutters.

"Kayla!" Principal Axelrod says brightly. "You're a leader in your class. The other girls look up to you, and I know you've organized some class get-togethers on Shabbos." Kayla looks mollified, though still wary. "And Aviva, you're wonderfully creative. I've seen some of your projects in school—especially your science fair entry last year. I think, together, the two of you could find a way to get your grade excited about the Bas Mitzvah Bash."

"*Together?*" I echo Principal Axelrod dubiously.

Kayla sounds equally horrified. "With *her?*" She straightens. "I don't work with Aviva Jacobs. Everyone knows that. Even our teachers won't pair us up."

I would be offended if she weren't totally right about that. "We're a *bad* match, Principal Axelrod," I protest. "We're not going to get anyone excited. *We're* not even excited for it. Can't we just play machanayim?"

Principal Axelrod gives us a quelling look. "You *will* work together," she says. "I know you have it in you." Kayla opens her mouth to protest, and Principal Axelrod says dryly, "And I remind you that this isn't a reward. It's a consequence of your actions." Kayla's mouth snaps shut again.

Principal Axelrod beams at us, once again grandmotherly. "Wonderful. Let's meet on Thursday at lunch to see what you've come up with."

Thursday at lunch. That's when machanayim tryouts are. "Fine," Kayla grinds out, and she stalks out of the office.

For once, I'm stalking right beside her.

Chapter 4

EMA DOESN'T NEED TO KNOW I got in trouble. The school rarely calls her when I get sent to the office. Everyone seems to know instinctively that Ema has enough to deal with without bringing me into the mix, and it's not like *being disruptive* is enough of a reason to call someone's mother. I don't talk back or anything like that, not on purpose.

This time is maybe a little worse than other times, and I feel a twinge of guilt when I think about Rikki's purple face. I even consider calling Rikki to see how she's doing, but I think about having to identify myself as the one who threw the ball, and I don't have the courage to do it. But it wasn't intentional. I didn't even want to hurt Kayla like that. And I've been *punished* anyway.

I'm full of dread when I think about having to plan something with Kayla. And not just *something*—something the whole grade is angry about having in the first place. We're going to fail no matter what we do.

I want to complain to Ema, to let her know all about how I'm missing the machanayim game and it isn't *fair*; it's the thing I'm *best* at and now I'm going to do something I'm terrible at instead.

But when I come home, the words escape me. Ema is standing

outside, which is an unusual sight for an ordinary afternoon. I can see a newly delivered package untouched beside our door, waiting for me to bring it inside, but Ema has moved it over so she could emerge from the apartment. She's carefully putting little signs up along the path to the mikvah. Earlier today, the sidewalk in front of the shul was repaved, wet cement laid down across it, and Ema has gotten signs to put in the grass that point people toward the mikvahs and away from the wet cement. She's crouched down, her hair wrapped in a shiny green tichel headscarf and her gaze on some muddy ground that is keeping her from getting a sign in properly.

She jams it in again, lips pursed in frustration, and then she notices me standing at the end of the path. "Aviva!" she says, smiling, and her eyes glow, her face as pretty as it is in the old wedding album she keeps hidden away in a box under her bed. My desire to complain disappears. It's so *rare* that Ema smiles, and I duck my head and run to her, helping her stick the sign into the mud.

"The cement will be dry by morning," Ema says. "But the men coming to daven tonight at the shul won't be able to see that the sidewalk is wet." She motions to another row of signs along the other end of the path, already up. "And I'm expecting Mrs. Reisman tonight."

I brighten. It's always a treat to watch her son, Gavi. "How was your day?" Ema asks as we stack up the boxes and go inside. We climb the narrow staircase inside the mikvah that leads to our apartment, hands running against the scratchy white wall, and I can smell sesame chicken and rice cooking inside, waiting for me. I put down the boxes, opening them to pull out the food inside of them and move it to the pantry.

Ema seems to relax once we're inside, quiet tension fading away as soon as I realize that it's there. I exhale, the same tension leaving me. "It was fine," I lie, and then I remember I have something I can tell her. "They announced that the Bas Mitzvah Bash this year is a mother-daughter event. It'll still be at the arcade, but there's also going to be singing and dancing. And Principal Axelrod asked Kayla Eisenberger and me to help with more ideas to get people excited." I don't mention that it was a punishment.

"Oh."

Ema looks taken aback, suddenly overwhelmed, and I say quickly, "You don't have to go. You have a lot of work to do at the mikvah, and you might be busy that day—"

Ema is still staring at me, at a loss, and I feel guilty for bringing it up. "I don't even want to go," I say, and I roll my eyes. "Why should I give up a perfectly good Sunday on *school*?"

Ema squeezes her eyes shut and turns around, opening the oven and reaching in for the pan of chicken. "Of course . . . of course we'll go," she says, and then lets out a hiss of pain as her bare fingers touch the hot pan. I pass her a towel, alarmed, and Ema takes the pan out and then hurries to the sink to run her fingers under water. "It's your Bas Mitzvah," she says quietly. "You aren't going to miss it."

"We can decide later," I offer, wishing I never said anything. It will be like the Chanukah play we had last year, when I got to play Judah the Maccabee. Ema was so excited for me, so enthusiastic, but on the night before the play, she got sick. She spent the night pale and vomiting, and I begged her not to go in the end. I messed up my lines onstage and started laughing and wasn't able to stop until I ran offstage. When I got home, I told Ema that I got a stand-ing ovation. (I also spent the night cleaning up a flood that the dyb-buk started in the laundry room, but that was a nice distraction.)

Ema doesn't do well outside. "Actually," I say, remembering my walk with Mrs. Leibowitz. "There was something else too. Mrs. Leibowitz asked if I could babysit for a few hours Monday night. She'd bring me there and home," I say hastily. "You won't have to leave the mikvah. And the kids will be asleep most of the time, so I can do my homework—"

Ema stops moving. She's spooning out the chicken on to the rice, and her hand freezes, then seizes up. My heartbeat quickens, and I can't look at her. I turn to the staircase, where I can see the dybbuk hovering just down the steps. "I don't want you out at night," she says.

My own hands tremble. "I won't be *out*, I'll be in Mrs. Leibow-itz's house. She lives two blocks away. And she thinks I'm respon-sible enough to watch her kids—"

Ema's smile looks strained now. "Maybe you can help her out another time," she suggests. "During the day, or if she needs an extra hand when she's home. But you aren't doing this." Her voice is firm.

"She said she'd pay me ten dollars an hour—" I try, but Ema is already shaking her head.

"No, Aviva," she says, and her voice brooks no argument. There is a dangerous wavering note to the way she says my name, and that silences me more than the *no* does.

I want to stamp my foot. It isn't *fair*, not when Mrs. Leibow-itz thinks I *can* do it, not when plenty of other kids my age are babysitting. I'll be babysitting *tonight* for Mrs. Reisman's son, and I'm not like Ema. I don't *want* to stay at home for the rest of my life—

But I swallow my objections. At school, I might have a big mouth, but Ema isn't like Morah Miller or Kayla. Ema won't shrug it off or send me out for a walk or yell right back at me.

I have to see the school social worker twice a week during lunchtime, I guess because of Abba. Mostly, we play word games and talk about the dybbuk. But she's the one who gave me a word for why Ema doesn't do what other adults do. Not *crazy* but *depressed*. I hate the word. It's the kind of thing that my classmates groan when they flunk tests or don't get to go anywhere during winter vacation. *I'm so depressed.*

Ema isn't *so depressed*. Ema's just . . . different. We're okay just the way we are, like we've always been. We don't need fancy names or doctors to tell us that we aren't fine. And I know what Ema needs: me, not giving her a reason to shut down again. Not giving her a reason for her eyes to cloud over and her face to get stiff like she isn't really here anymore. I'm all Ema has, and I can't push her.

Instead, I blink away sudden, frustrated tears and eat my dinner in silence.

Ema eats silently too, her fork moving mechanically from her plate to her mouth, sometimes without anything on it. She used to do that before, when Abba would laugh at it and say, "Shoshie, you're meant to eat the food," and I would laugh with Abba. Now, it leaves a pit of fear weighing down my stomach.

I'm relieved when the doorbell chimes. Mrs. Reisman has arrived at the mikvah.

Her son, Gavi, is just about two, all big eyes and dirty fingernails and the lingering smell of applesauce, and he lets out a squeal when he sees me. "Gavi and Avi, together again," Mrs. Reisman says, shaking her head ruefully. "Are you sure you're okay with him tagging along?"

Gavi is already in my arms, giggling as I spin him around. He puts his chubby little fingers on my face, pinching my nose, and he says, "Beep!"

I tweak his nose. "Boing," I say, and he giggles. Mrs. Reisman shakes her head again, smiling, and she moves to the counter to write out a check for the mikvah.

I can feel a presence behind me before I turn, and I sigh, suddenly aware that Gavi and I are being watched. "Not *now*, dybbuk," I mutter, but of course he's already there.

He's hovering in the hallway near the laundry room, and I hurry over to it, just in time to see he's dropped a red velvet chair cover from the shul in with the mikvah's white towels. "No," I hiss, yanking it out and hoping it was soon enough. The dybbuk just laughs silently, Gavi squirming out of my arms.

The dybbuk is a boy just my age, though I think he's always been my age. Maybe he's been growing up with me, I don't know. He has brown hair and olive skin, a little darker than mine and much darker than Ema's pale coloring. When he laughs, sometimes I can't tell if it's with me or at me.

In that way, being around the dybbuk is kind of like being

around my classmates. I throw the red chair cover at him, and it passes right through him, landing on the floor. "Try to behave for *once,*" I snap at him, and the dybbuk laughs, somersaulting through the air and vanishing again.

I look around for more damage. Gavi is climbing into the laundry basket. He tips it over so it's on his head, and I let him run around the waiting room, banging into chairs and laughing harder and harder each time. Ema is sitting behind the desk, carefully putting away Mrs. Reisman's check in the flat metal cash box that sits in the top drawer, and the dybbuk is lurking near her, eyeing the check speculatively.

I remember how embarrassed Ema was the last time the dybbuk tore up a check, and I glare at him warningly. He snickers, swooping forward to the spare bathroom, and I leave Gavi behind for a minute and follow him to it.

He's turned on the bathtub and stopped the drain, and I yank out the stopper before he does much damage. Some days are like this, when the dybbuk seems to feed off of my bad mood and wreaks extra havoc. I can't sit still for a minute.

I stomp from the spare bathroom and return to Gavi, who is climbing the stairs to the apartment. Our apartment is a small little trio of rooms, two bedrooms and a kitchen with a table for Shabbos meals, but we have a few toys left over from when I was little. "Come on, Gavi," I say. "I'll show you my Magna-Tiles."

I pull them out, clapping two tiles together. Gavi loves it. "Look," I say, sticking a third tile on top of the first two. "A bird." I flap the first two tiles.

Gavi claps them together. "Bud," he proclaims joyfully.

I set up another four squares, forming a 3D square. "Want to build a house?"

Gavi's hand slams down on my house, shattering it. "Bud!" he says again.

"Okay, okay." I set up another three tiles, these triangular. "Bat," I suggest.

Gavi pouts at my bat. "Bud," he corrects me.

"Yessir." I add a few more tiles. "Ostrich."

Gavi giggles. "Doggie!" he declares at the mass of tiles. I shake my head. I'll never understand babies.

When we go back downstairs, Ema has disappeared into the mikvah. I hear her voice, low and concerned. "Did you speak to the rabbi about the temporary filling?" she's saying.

"I completely forgot." Mrs. Reisman sounds embarrassed. "I can call him now—"

"Take your time," Ema says gently. "It happens."

I take a quick inventory of the waiting room, searching for the dybbuk's latest prank. Last week, he soaped up the entire floor of the waiting room with a bar of soap and some water, and poor Mrs. Feigenbaum nearly slipped. One time, he swapped the nail polish remover with the lens solution and Mrs. Cohn had to get a ride home because her contact lenses were ruined. You can never be too careful with the dybbuk when he's in a mood.

I don't see anything, though, and I lift Gavi into my arms and settle on a chair with one of the board books that Mrs. Reisman brought along. "Oink, quack, la dee da," I recite from memory. "The pig goes oink!"

The phone rings. I don't pick up. Ema always says to let it go to machine. "The sheep goes baa." I baa. Gavi baas. "Three little ducks say—"

The machine picks up the call, and I quiet Gavi for a moment, listening. It's a man on the phone, sounding very embarrassed. "I'm sorry to bother you, Mrs.—Ms.—" He stumbles and then gives up on a title for Ema altogether. "I noticed there are signs on the way to the shul, but they're, ah . . ." He clears his throat. "They seem to be pointing people toward the wet cement—"

"*Dybbuk*," I growl out, irritated. "*Why?*" He's there beside me suddenly, peering down at the singing pigs with interest. I swat at him, and my hand goes right through him. "Hold on, Gavi," I mutter. "We have to run outside for a minute."

I hurry outside, over to where the signs have been arranged in a line. The *THIS WAY* and the arrows are all pointing toward the line of wet cement, and I pluck them out, jamming them back into the paths toward the mikvah and the shul. Gavi stays cuddled in my arm, poking me with one of the signs as I set up the rest, and I put the last sign down beside the cement, scowling down at it.

There's a strange shape in the wet cement, and I squint down at it. It's a little like a jagged, thin pinwheel. I have the strangest feeling I've seen it before, but I can't remember when or where. Did the dybbuk draw it into the cement?

I bite my lip. It's dark outside, and I can't see anything but the dim light at the front of the mikvah. I feel an odd shiver pass through me, an unease I can't shake, and I hurry inside past a newly delivered package with Gavi, drawn back to the familiarity of the sound of splashing and Ema's voice calling, "Kosher!" from inside the mikvah.

Chapter 5

I'M DREAMING OF THE DARK, OF hard pavement and sneering laughs, of screams and sobbing and sirens in the distance. Someone is calling my name, but I don't answer, and there are hazy faces in front of me, shaking me. I don't move.

I wake up, still shaking from the dream, the sirens still blaring in the back of my mind. *Wait.* That wasn't a dream. There are sirens outside of my window.

I sit up abruptly, my heart pounding, and I call, "Ema?" No answer.

"Ema?" I say again, climbing out of bed. There is a nasty feeling in my throat, like a lump that won't dislodge. It'll just get bigger and bigger until it takes up my whole throat and I can't breathe or talk or cry, and I—

I rub my eyes and push that thought away, wandering through our tiny apartment in search of Ema. She's nowhere to be found. Her coffee mug is on the table, her siddur lying on the counter like she ran off in a hurry, and I feel another prickle of fear. "Ema!" I call, and I dress in a hurry, pulling on my long blue uniform skirt and a gray polo.

I'm hurrying down the stairs, pushing past the dybbuk's grim face, and I can hear the noise from outside even louder now. I tear out of the door into chaos.

The police are here, parked in front of the shul. I stand at the door, frozen in horror, and all I can think about is Ema—if she's in trouble, if she's *gone*—

I can't think at first, my brain fuzzy and my breath coming out in too-short bursts. I can hear my pulse like horses clip-clopping against my ears. *Clop. Clop. Clopclopclop.* It's too rapid, and suddenly it's too hard to breathe at all. I suck air in and it sounds like a hiccup, like a little choked moan. The world is fuzzy around me like it was in my dream, and I open my mouth but words don't come out.

Something passes through me. It feels like a strange warmth, and everything is blurry again until I see the dybbuk in front of me. He moved through me as if I wasn't there at all, and I glare at his back, annoyance replacing my panic. I can breathe again, and I manage to turn back to watch the crowd in front of the shul.

There is a sea of men around the police officers, dressed in black davening jackets and white shirts, and for a moment, the crowd shifts and I see a flash of Ema. She stands at the center of the waves of men like Moses at the Red Sea, her arms tight around herself as she speaks to the police officers.

I walk forward, gripped by an unnamable terror, and I hear the men as they speak. "Unacceptable!" someone is saying. "This isn't the first incident—"

"No," a police officer says grimly. "We've been working with Beacon Shomrim—"

"It's not enough!" someone else says hotly. He's supporting a stooped elderly man—Mrs. Feigenbaum's husband, I recognize from Shabbos at the shul—who looks frail and cold as he stares down at the pavement.

No, I realize suddenly. Not the pavement, exactly. They're all crowded around the wet cement, now dry in the morning sun, and I drag myself closer to see what it is that has everyone so shaken. The crowd of men don't part for me, and I don't push into them, even though I want to. Instead, I circle the crowd, peering in from the side.

Ema is standing opposite the police officers on the grass between the sidewalk and the men. She has the same frailness to her expression as Mr. Feigenbaum does, but she stands stiffly, brittle but tall and very pale. "It has to be fixed," she says quietly.

"It will be," one police officer assures her. "First thing today. We've already put in a call."

"We'll keep someone posted here tonight," another officer says in a low, soothing tone, and she reaches out to put a hand on Ema's arm. Ema doesn't react. "These things happen. Probably just a teenager feeling edgy." The officer rolls her eyes. "Nothing to worry about."

I crane my neck, trying to see what they're all looking at. It's what I saw last night—the thin, jagged pinwheel shape in the cement, now dried into the sidewalk in front of the shul. Like this, it looks so familiar that it jolts something inside of me, and I am shaky, my vision blurring for a minute, and my mind goes blissfully blank before I can put a name to the symbol I'm seeing.

I wonder again if the dybbuk did it, if he put this shape in the sidewalk and left dozens of people confused and afraid. But when I look back at the door to the mikvah, still ajar, I see him standing there. He looks just like Ema looks, like I feel: unnerved and afraid, brought to this only by a strange symbol on the sidewalk.

▰▰▰

At school, our morning drama is the only thing that anyone is talking about, in whispers and hushed voices. Avital says something that I don't quite catch, but it has Elisheva and Shira both shrinking back, wide-eyed. "I don't want to, like, talk about *that*," Shira says, shivering. "It gets me so freaked out—"

"We *should* talk about it," Avital argues, but Shira is already turning away, moving to Kayla and her group on the other side of the room.

"You know my cousin Eli?" Kayla is saying, shaking her head gravely. "He said there's a kid in his class who was walking from Beacon into New Beacon and a bunch of kids jumped him." She lowers her voice for dramatic effect. "*They cut off his tzitzis!*" she says, and a few girls gasp.

I sit on my desk, absently winding and unwinding the cold, metal lever that opens the window as I stare outside. There's a police car parked in front of the school today, and the preschool kids are waving at the police officer from the playground. "My mother never lets my sisters walk from Beacon to school," Esther says from behind me, smoothing her shirt down where she tucks it into her skirt. "She says it's much too dangerous. You never know—"

"Remember what happened back when..." Ariella's high voice trails off, and she turns to look at me for a moment. "Is it true that you *saw the swastika?*" she asks, her eyes wide. "My father said you were right there this morning."

I blink owlishly, taken aback by the name thrust at me that I can put to the jagged pinwheel on the ground. *Swastika.* I recognize the word from books, from stories told by Morah Miller about a time period that feels forever ago now. I know it's *bad*, and I know I've never seen one in Beacon before.

My arms feel too stiff at my sides, cumbersome and awkward as everyone turns to me. Yesterday's machanayim mishap seems all but forgotten, and my classmates crowd around me, asking a dozen questions at once in a cacophony of curiosity.

"What did it look like?"

"Was there anyone there?"

"Are they going to get rid of it?"

"Did you see anything?"

Usually, I enjoy being the center of attention. But I blink again, as overwhelmed as Ema must have felt when she was surrounded this morning, and I stutter, unsure what to respond. I'm saved by Morah Miller, briskly opening the door to the room and clearing her throat.

Everyone scurries to stand by their seats, and I exhale, relieved without knowing why. I don't want to talk about it, that much I know. By the time recess comes, at least, the class is distracted again. Weird marks on the sidewalk can only keep us busy for so long. Rikki is in the other sixth-grade class, and she's come up to the roof for machanayim, a crowd of girls around her.

"My nose is fine," she says, making a face. "I just have to keep this weird pinching bandage on it for a few weeks." She taps it where someone has already drawn a glittery pink heart on the bandage in gel pen. "And the swelling's already going down, see?"

I don't see it. The other girls are bobbing their heads admiringly, though, so I nod and smile and say, "I'm—I'm really sorry about—"

Rikki heaves a sigh. "It's *fine*," she says, and she smirks. "I like getting to say that I was the last one out in a machanayim game with the two of you." She gestures at me and at Kayla, who is standing awkwardly on her other side. Kayla looks just as uncomfortable as me, and she undoes her ponytail and winds her scrunchie around it again as Rikki goes on. "I can't believe the principal kicked you two out of the big game, though. We might have actually had a *chance* with you two."

"It's not fair," Esther is quick to agree. "It was an accident. And see? Rikki's okay!" The other girls burst into noises of solidarity, mostly around Kayla. Still, I watch them, bemused. I don't think I've ever had so many of my classmates on my side for something.

"Ugh," Kayla complains. "And instead, I have to work on this year's *terrible* Bas Mitzvah Bash. As if losing machanayim wasn't punishment enough." She curls her lip. "Or working with *Aviva*."

This time, no one laughs except Shira with a strident titter, and there are a few uncomfortable glances at me. Kayla's freckled face is stubborn, and I scowl at her, hurt despite my best efforts not to care. "I don't want to work with you either."

We glare at each other, the girls around us watching as though we might start hurling machanayim balls at each other again. Instead, Kayla says, "Well, we *have* to. So . . ."

"So," I echo, the reality of our situation setting in. I don't know what Principal Axelrod will do if we don't have any ideas by Thursday afternoon. But I can guess, and every guess I have ends in one place. "Principal Axelrod is going to call my mother if we don't come up with a plan," I say gloomily. I don't mean to—not to Kayla, who would be happy to see me in trouble, who would probably shrug off my worries and insist I deserve them.

But Kayla's expression shifts, and she looks almost guilty for a moment. "Yeah," she agrees. "Your mother doesn't need to hear about . . ." She shifts, yanking me away from the crowd, and I remember that Kayla's mother used to be super close with my mother. When we were kids, we'd spend all of our time together, the four of us and our fathers. Back when I had a father and a best friend. "My mother says she was the one to see the symbol on the sidewalk first."

This is the most civil conversation we've had in years. "She wasn't," I admit. "I saw it last night before anyone." Kayla looks dubiously at me, and I tell her what the dybbuk did. "I didn't know what it was," I mumble self-consciously. "So I didn't tell anyone. I didn't realize."

"Yeah." Kayla's brow furrows. "How do you know that it's really a—that you have a *dybbuk* in your house?"

"He isn't in my house. He's in the mikvah—" I wave my hands, frustrated. It's a lost cause. "Never mind." I change the topic. "What are we going to do about Principal Axelrod?"

Kayla bites her lip. "I guess we should meet up tonight and come up with some ideas," she says reluctantly.

I stiffen at the thought. Ema will never let me go out to Kayla's house, but I don't want Kayla in my tiny little apartment or the mikvah below. When Kayla and I were friends, I lived in one of the apartments down on Spruce Street, with their big bedrooms and living rooms with picture windows letting the sun stream in. My apartment now has little space, especially in my bedroom, and I can't imagine a third person fitting into it even for a few hours.

I don't want to explain any of that to Kayla. "Fine," I say, frowning at her. "Come over after dinner."

Kayla scoffs. "No. You come to me. You have *criminals* at your house."

I glare at her. "I *can't*," I say. "My mother works in the mikvah at night, remember? She can't drive me to your house." She doesn't even have a car. We haven't had one in years. "You'll have to come over to my house."

Kayla's eyes narrow, our tiny truce already fading. "I will not."

"Then I'll tell Principal Axelrod that it's your fault we don't have anything," I shoot back.

"You're such a *jerk*," Kayla snaps. "Everyone in this school gives you special treatment, and you don't deserve any of it. Like you're the only one who's ever had something bad—" She stops, her jaw clenching.

As though *this* is special treatment instead of a miserable punishment. Kayla likes to pretend that I chose this, that I want to be treated like an outsider. Kayla is the class princess. As if she knows *anything* about me. I fume silently, my feet tap-tapping against the ground while I wait for Kayla to give in.

I know she will. We don't have another choice. *"Fine."* Kayla makes a face. "Ugh."

"Ugh yourself," I snap, already beginning to regret my decision. Principal Axelrod is a less intimidating enemy than Kayla Eisenberger.

At least Principal Axelrod isn't a *bully*.

Chapter 6

"NURIT," EMA MURMURS.

"Shoshie." Kayla and I linger beside our mothers, staring at each other and joining, for an instant, in cringing at the awkwardness between them. Kayla's mother has always been kind of intimidating, a much stricter eighth-grade teacher at Beacon TDS who wasn't nearly as popular as Ema was. But they were best friends, inseparable in the hallways and a mystery to their students. Ema was every student's confidant, outgoing and motherly. Mrs. Eisenberger is severe and off-putting in school, stern with her students while they crave her approval.

I remember her differently, of course—Kayla's mother, quick to smile at home and affectionate with Kayla. She was scary-stern, but the kind of scary-stern I trusted. Now, though, she stands uncertainly by the door to the mikvah, lurking as though she can't wait to get away but also can't bring herself to leave. She's tall, still dressed in a sweater over a straight black skirt, every bit as formal as she is in school. Ema is nearly her height but slight enough that she looks bony next to Mrs. Eisenberger, and she's wearing a dull gray tichel and a thin shirt that makes her look underdressed for their exchange. Mrs. Eisenberger doesn't sweep her eyes over Ema like she does girls who are out in the hall during class time, only shifts and toys with a bracelet on her wrist. "I saw you have a patrol car outside," she offers.

Ema nods, smoothing her shirt down as though she heard what I was thinking. "Just until the cement dries," she says wryly.

"Good. That's . . . it's good they're on top of it," Mrs. Eisenberger says hastily. "That they're taking this seriously." She swallows, looking to Kayla suddenly as though she can't meet Ema's eyes.

Ema is tall and fragile and strong at once, and I stand next to her and listen as she says kindly, "And you parked right in front? Near the patrol car?" Mrs. Eisenberger nods, and Ema smiles. "Good," she says. "That's good."

Something tips over in the main bathroom. I hear it crash and I jolt, Kayla and her mother both jumping at the noise. "It's the dybbuk," I say apologetically. "I have to—"

I turn on my heel and hurry toward the bathroom, groaning when I see what the dybbuk has done. There was a handheld mirror among the toiletries, but the dybbuk must have hung it from the handheld shower handle, calculating that it would fall and flip the shower on at the same time. The showerhead was left on the bathroom floor, and it's twisting around wildly with the force of the water pressure, spraying water everywhere.

"Dybbuk!" I say, frustrated. The dybbuk is hovering at the open doorway into the mikvah room, grinning impishly. I charge through the spray, slipping and sliding on the water as it soaks my clothing. The dybbuk stares down at me, his face distorted by the water, and I kick off my shoes before they're completely ruined and dive for the showerhead.

Instead, I bang my own head on the sink and fall to the floor. The dybbuk comes close, patting my head with its ghostly hand and then vanishing an instant later, just as a voice says, "What are you *doing*?"

Kayla. She's staring into the room in alarm, and I gasp out, "Shut the door! The shower! Get—" Kayla blinks, slamming the door closed behind her. Machanayim reflexes mean that she does the same thing that I did—charges for the showerhead like she's charging for a machanayim ball. Since I'm right in front of the sink, she manages to avoid the head-banging part and wrestles with the showerhead, finally flicking it off.

We're both soaked, shell-shocked on the ground. Kayla says, her voice high, "Did the dybbuk *really* do that?"

I nod silently.

The bathroom door opens again. This time, it's Ema standing on the other side of it, taking in Kayla and me as we blink up at her. I'm sopping wet, curled on the bathroom floor as water drips from the sink onto my head. Kayla is inside the bathtub, her reddish hair scraggly and damp in her scrunchie, and her shirt soaking.

"I'll clean up," I say sheepishly.

Ema nods, very slowly. "We aren't expecting any visitors tonight," she says. I wince, remembering my excuse for why I couldn't go to Kayla's house. "I'm going to go up to bed." She waves a finger at me. "Don't do anything I wouldn't do."

"But that's everything," I say under my breath. Ema doesn't hear me, but Kayla does, and she wiggles her eyebrows at me. I give her a *look*. Kayla presses her lips together and doesn't quite smile, even if her eyes glitter. It's strange, sharing a secret joke with Kayla, when we've shared so little for so many years.

Ema sighs. "Be careful, Aviva. Don't open the door for *anyone*. If the police officer comes to the door, come and get me." I nod obediently. Ema steps into the flooded bathroom, moving gingerly to me, and she kneels for a moment to press a kiss to my forehead. She picks her way out again, looking back at Kayla and me for another moment, and she says, her voice wistful, "It's nice to see you again, Kayla."

"You too," Kayla says, and she smiles like she means it. The smile fades again once Ema is gone, and she hisses at me, "If this is a practical joke—"

"It's *not*. I mean, it is, but it isn't mine." I wave helplessly at the doorway, where the dybbuk is lurking again. "You can't see the dybbuk, can you?"

Kayla looks blankly where I'm gesturing. "So this mikvah really is haunted? That's what you're going with?" But she doesn't sound quite as annoyed anymore. "How do you know?"

I tell her about the soap on the floor, about Mrs. Blumstein's candies, and about the time the dybbuk pulled me out of the mikvah. Kayla stops me then, her eyes wide. "Wait," she says. "Like, *in* the mikvah? You went inside?" Her voice is hushed, and I remember that for lots of kids my age, even the idea of a mikvah is something beyond us. Our mothers don't discuss it with us, and we're not supposed to ask.

"Just once," I say, self-conscious. "It's just—it's right *there*." I point at the open door to the mikvah. "See?"

Kayla climbs out of the bathtub, slipping a little as she tiptoes across the floor toward the mikvah room. "Whoa," she says, peering inside. "It looks like a pool."

"It is a pool. There's chlorine in it and everything. But the water comes from a well in the ground. Or something like that." I point out an opening on the side of the mikvah. "From there, see? Then it empties out again on the other side somewhere." I squint, trying to find the opening on the bottom of the mikvah. "Some of it is drained and refilled every day, and the chlorine and pH levels are checked before each visitor goes in." I have no idea what a pH level is, but I feel very intelligent, parroting Ema's explanations.

Kayla squints into it. "How many people go inside every night?"

I shrug, bashful. "Not so many here. Each woman only goes in once a month, tops. After their . . . you know. Their period."

Kayla leans forward, her voice hushed and a little smug. "I've gotten mine, you know. Last month. Remember that day I left school early? I went to the bathroom, and I thought I was *dying* before I realized." We giggle together nervously. At the beginning of the year, the school social worker came into our class to give us a lecture on the *changes that were happening to our bodies*. We all squirmed and laughed and tried to talk as little about it as possible.

Kayla's eyes are bright as she looks at the mikvah. "So once I'm married, I'm going to be dipping in here every month? While someone *watches*?" I lift my shoulders and drop them, uncomfortable again. That's the part of the mikvah I like to think about the least. Kayla wrinkles her nose. "Ew. No offense, but I'm going to go to a different mikvah. One where *no one* knows me." She says it with the authority of someone who's already gotten her period. "And it's supposed to make you . . . like, holy, right?"

"I guess so." I remember the one time I ventured into the mikvah, the sleepy sensation that washed over me before the dybbuk had jolted me back from drowning. "Or . . . pure, I think. Clean."

"Huh." Kayla squints at the water. "Does it feel different than other water?" She contemplates the mikvah with keen interest. I can only mumble something noncommittal in response. I've never thought too deeply about the mikvah. The excitement has always been in the visitors to our quiet evenings, not in the actual pool.

Kayla sees it differently. "It's like magic water," she muses. "And it's just for *them*. *Us*, someday. Nearly every woman in Beacon dips into a—" She stops, probably realizing at that moment what I already know. My mother isn't married anymore. This grand rite for women doesn't include her.

I don't want to think about Ema, guiding all these women into a mikvah where she'll never dip. I nod abruptly. "We will too, someday," I say. "Just like everyone else." I see the ripple of excitement on Kayla's face at the idea. The mikvah is an exclusive hideaway for women, a well-kept secret place where no one else would ever dare to venture.

Well, except for us right now.

Kayla watches me for a moment, and she says suddenly, "Let's go inside."

"What?" I stare at her, then at the water. I still remember my first time in the water with unease, like there's something to it that I forgot. What I might have forgotten, I can't imagine. The feeling of the dybbuk pulling my hand out of the pool is still burned into my mind. It's the only time the dybbuk has ever actually touched me instead of passing through me.

Kayla doesn't know any of this. She's looking at the water with her eyes narrowed, and she says, "Come on. You have a *magic pool* in your house. We're already soaking wet. Let's go in. Unless you're scared," she challenges me. "What, do you think you'll get in trouble?"

"No," I say, immediately on the defensive. "I told you, I did it before."

Kayla shrugs out of her wet skirt, unbuttoning her uniform polo and pulling it over her head. She's left in her underwear, and she tilts her head, daring me to do the same.

I scowl at her. "If you drown, I'm going to tell everyone it was your idea," I say, yanking off my uniform as well.

Kayla just grins daringly. "I'll tell everyone you pulled me down," she retorts, pulling down her knee-high socks. "They'd believe it too, after yesterday."

I peel my own socks off, deciding not to point out that if she *drowns*, she isn't telling anyone anything. The thought of it—of watching someone's eyes turn sightless in front of me, of seeing someone fade away—makes my stomach twist. I look up to catch the dybbuk's eyes again before I can breathe, and then I roll my eyes at Kayla. "It was just machanayim," I say. "You didn't have to be so nasty about the Bas Mitzvah Bash. I'm not even going." Probably.

Kayla wrinkles her brow. "What do you mean? You'd *better* go.

They rearranged the whole stupid event for you and your mother." She sounds deeply resentful again.

"We didn't *ask* for that," I say. "My mother . . . Ema isn't going to go. She doesn't really go anywhere." I try to sound casual when I say that, as though this is an ordinary, shame-free fact. "She's not into this stuff." *This stuff*, like going to school events or parent-teacher conferences or even the supermarket. My aunt Raizy comes in every summer and takes me back-to-school shopping for new clothes. She tries to persuade Ema to move to Milwaukee and be with family, but Ema and I don't want to leave Beacon. It's the last place Abba . . .

I don't think Ema would make it to the airport without getting sick anyway.

Kayla scoffs. She turns to the mikvah, focused on it as though it's a mountain to climb, and she gingerly sticks a foot inside. "It's warm," she says, startled. "I didn't think it would be warm."

"Yeah. Like a big bath." I watch her descend. There's a care to her movements, a reverence as her fingers touch the water. "Does it feel magical?" I say, half-kidding. "Are you all cleansed now?"

"Maybe," Kayla says smugly, her tone of awe at the mikvah replaced with more familiar mischief. Without missing a beat, she propels herself off of the steps, treading water in place like she's in a pool.

"Come on, coward," Kayla taunts me. "Come inside."

I step down carefully. I'm not Kayla, looking to some distant future where we'll be the ones going into the mikvah. Instead, I drift to the past, my old memories of the mikvah returning. The dybbuk seized my arm—*there*, when I was much smaller, when this seemed so much deeper and larger. Now, I can float over to the other corner of the pool in a matter of seconds.

I dip a little, and Kayla catches my arm like the dybbuk did. "Careful," she says. "It's kind of nice in here." We bob together, almost smiling, and Kayla says abruptly, "I bet your mother would come to the Bash."

I shake my head. It doesn't matter. Ema won't come, and I probably won't either, and that'll be it. "Well, you'd better come," Kayla says again, scowling at me. "Whatever we do is going to flop, and I'm not going to be the only one there to watch everyone complaining about it. I don't *fail* at things." She leans back against the mikvah wall. "It's a shame we can't make it a pool party," she says wistfully. "Or a haunting. Your dybbuk could create all kinds of chaos."

"Don't give him any ideas," I say, rolling my eyes. He isn't in the mikvah room right now, but I know he's around here somewhere, listening in. "The arcade is great. We just . . . we just need to excite people somehow."

Kayla sighs. "No one's going to be excited about the same old thing, but without our . . ." Her voice trails off, and I stare at the wall of the mikvah, reading the plaque with the blessing over and over again. This might not be a real immersion, but Kayla and I are talking like we don't hate each other, and that's a blessing in itself.

"Hey," Kayla says suddenly, "is this where the water drains out of?" She's kicking something on the wall with her toe. I shrug. She gives me a look of exasperation and then dives into the water headfirst, knocking my legs aside and tracing something I can't see with her fingers.

I peer down after her, angling back as Kayla emerges from the water. "There's a drain," she reports. "But there's something else. Look." I go down too, unwilling to be called a coward again.

The mikvah water is warm and blue around me, and I blink as the chlorine stings my eyes and squint at what it is Kayla has seen.

There is a drain at the bottom of the far wall, just like I said. But in the corner is an odd rectangle, a dark outline almost as long as me, beginning just below water level. And on it, I can see a tiny, silver handle.

I come back up, coughing out chlorine as it burns my nostrils and throat, and I find Kayla waiting. "You saw it too, didn't you?" she says.

"A door," I say, and my heart skips a beat. A mysterious door inside the pool, one Ema has never mentioned. Maybe she doesn't know about it either. Maybe no one does, except for Kayla and me. "There's a secret door in the mikvah."

Chapter 7

KAYLA HAS TO GO HOME WEARING my dry clothes, a little too long and tight enough that we both hear the cracking sound of a few snapped threads at the waistband when she pulls them on, and neither of us comes up with anything to spice up the Bas Mitzvah Bash. Still, it feels like it was a good night, and I wake up cheerful the next morning.

"Ema?" I call, stepping into the kitchen. I hear a movement from her bedroom, and I poke my head inside, my good mood fading. Ema is curled up in bed, staring blankly out at the wall of her room. It happens sometimes. Ema has good days and bad, and I avert my eyes. I don't like seeing her on the bad days. It leaves my stomach churning and a sense that I'm abandoning her when I go to school, even though it's what she'd want me to do. "I never want you to be like me," Ema whispered to me once, and I was horrified but also a tiny bit relieved.

Maybe it makes me horrible, to want something more than these cramped four walls. I wish sometimes that Ema would be the kind of mother who would walk me to school or hide her bad days away from sight, and that *definitely* makes me horrible. Ema does everything she can for me, and I can't let myself get lost in comparing it to what my classmates get from their mothers. Their mothers haven't gone through a quarter of what my mother has, and I'm not ungrateful enough to ever give voice to my most selfish thoughts about Ema.

Instead, I close her door quietly and pad out into the kitchen. I pick out the hard blue plastic bowls we use for dairy foods and pour myself a bowl of a sugary off-brand cereal, balancing the bowl on the steps downstairs so I won't spill the milk. The dybbuk is opening all the drawers of the desk in the waiting room when I come down, but he floats over to me to sit beside me as I eat my cereal. "Hi," I say, and I'm just glad to be talking to someone. "Did I imagine it, or did Kayla and I really kind of have a good time last night?"

The dybbuk grins at me, and I grin back, focusing on his smile instead of on Ema, wrapped in her heavy lavender comforter for what will probably be the rest of the day.

But the last of my good mood evaporates as soon as I get to school. Kayla is sitting with Shira, absorbed in the story she's telling, and she barely looks at me before she turns back to Shira. I frown. For a moment, I thought that we kind of became friends.

I guess not.

I take my usual spot at the window, perching on my desk and staring out. My desk rocks back and forth as I tap my feet, making a rhythmic noise against the floor, and Shira says, annoyed, "Could you cut that out? We're trying to have a conversation here." Kayla glances up at her words. She sees me watching her and then looks away.

I sigh. We're still going to have to get along for long enough to come up with a plan for the Bash. At least I know it's possible now.

Today is Thursday, which means machanayim tryouts and a meeting with Principal Axelrod. There's a ripple of excitement that passes through the classroom, everyone eager to try out for the machanayim team. "Do you think alternates get the team sweatshirt?" Esther wonders, tucking in her shirt as though in anticipation of it right now. We're only allowed to wear boring black zip-up sweatshirts in school with the logo at the corner of them, but the pullover team sweatshirt—with the school logo on the back with *BEACON TDS MACHANAYIM TEAM* around it in an arc—is the closest thing we have to a status symbol in school. Esther hates the uniform—wears colorful socks and big necklaces and headbands to accessorize as much as possible—and the sweatshirt would be another accessory for her.

"I don't care about that," Avital says, and she flashes her braces in a grin. "I just want to *play*." They both toss me a sidelong look. I keep my head high, refusing to look at anyone.

Morah Miller comes in, but she can't quite contain us today. We hurry through our davening and whisper to one another whenever she turns for a second, and she finally laughs and says, "Okay, girls. I see there's no teaching you today." Instead, we have conversations in Hebrew, stilted but enthusiastic.

I am paired with Esther, who only wants to talk about machanayim. "I'm sorry," she apologizes in Hebrew. "I wish you were playing. We all do."

"Maybe Principal Axelrod will change her mind," I say, but I don't really believe it. Rikki might be fine with us playing, but her face is still swollen and no one has forgotten that it's my fault.

It's a relief that I won't be able to go to the roof to watch the machanayim tryouts. I don't want to see what I'm missing. Instead, I walk alone to the principal's office. Kayla is behind me, walking through the empty hall, but she doesn't say anything to me.

We sit in Principal Axelrod's office, and I whisper to Kayla, "What are we going to do?" Kayla shrugs helplessly, still not meeting my eyes.

Principal Axelrod examines us from behind her desk, eyebrows raised and the scent of her perfume suddenly oppressive. I *like* her, I really do, but today I'm terrified that she's going to call my mother. And I can't—

"We have a plan," Kayla blurts out, her ears immediately going red. "A good one."

"Yeah," I agree immediately. "It's just . . . it's not quite ready yet. We need to work out the kinks."

"Right." Kayla bobs her head. "We can't explain it yet."

"We have to . . . organize." We're perfectly in sync, matching smiles on our faces, and Principal Axelrod doesn't buy it for a moment.

She sighs. "At least tell me that you're working on it," she says. We nod vigorously. Principal Axelrod sits back, satisfied. "We'll meet again next week," she decides. "Why don't you girls go upstairs and—"

"Can we try out?" Kayla says eagerly.

Principal Axelrod gives her a look. "—*watch* the tryouts?" she finishes, and Kayla slumps.

I don't go upstairs. I don't want to see any of it. Instead, I grab my lunch and wander down the hall to Mrs. Leibowitz's office, knocking on the door and waiting until she opens it for me.

"Aviva," she says, smiling. She motions me inside, a steaming coffee cup in one hand and a student's scrawled essay in the other. "I thought you'd be upstairs at machanayim tryouts."

"I'm not allowed to compete." I tell her the story, omitting the part where I might have been *really* angry when I threw the ball at Kayla. "Now I have to work on this Bas Mitzvah Bash." I look down at my hands.

Mrs. Leibowitz looks at me with something that seems suspiciously like pity, and I change the subject. "And my mother doesn't want me babysitting on Monday," I remember, a day late. "I'm sorry. I really did want to. We had a big fight about it."

Mrs. Leibowitz sets down the essay she was writing notes on in red pen and studies my expression. I cringe. I always say too much around Mrs. Leibowitz. "It's fine," I say quickly. "I don't want to upset Ema."

"Is your mother planning on coming to the Bas Mitzvah Bash?" Mrs. Leibowitz asks. I avoid her gaze. Ema said she would, but I don't think she really will. I can't imagine Ema outside of our house. It's like imagining Principal Axelrod at the beach. It just doesn't *fit*. Mrs. Leibowitz's eyes darken. "I see," she says.

I don't see anything. "I don't really want her there anyway," I try, scuffing my heels against the hard edges of the chair legs. "It'll be weird. All my friends will be there—" I stop, unable to keep up the fiction of *friends*. "I just . . . I don't think she'd enjoy it."

"Maybe she'll surprise you," Mrs. Leibowitz says heavily.

There's a knock at the door, a tentative noise that must be a student and not another teacher, and Mrs. Leibowitz nods to the girl peeking in from the window. I look up in surprise. It's Kayla, her lunch in hand and her face still flushed from the wind on the roof. "Hi," she says, biting her lip. "I didn't really want to watch the machanayim tryouts."

"I know what you mean," I say with a sigh. Kayla dawdles at the door, hesitant, and I nod to the empty chair next to me, impatient at the tension in the room. "Come on," I offer. "Sit down."

Kayla beams. "Thanks," she says, and she tosses a sidelong glance at Mrs. Leibowitz. Mrs. Leibowitz busies herself with something in her closet, digging through old papyrus and rolls of posters. "I always thought that it was so cool that you got to hang out in Mrs. Leibowitz's office," Kayla murmurs. "Do you always eat lunch here?"

"Usually." I don't tell her it's because I hate wandering around the lunchroom, searching for a table with friendly faces. Sometimes I would sit with other girls from my class, and they'd just look right past me, and I hate, *hate* being ignored. It's even worse when they welcome me to sit down and continue chatting with one another like I'm not here. When I open my mouth to speak, it's always when someone else starts talking too, and I get too loud so they can hear me.

The other girls don't know what to make of me, I guess. Maybe they feel bad for me because of Abba, and that feels even worse, like I'm just there because they pity me and not because they like me. Pity follows me around like a hanging storm cloud, impossible to overlook and impossible to confront, and I *never* eat in the lunchroom anymore. "I like it here. It's quiet."

Kayla takes that as a hint. "Oh. Sorry," she says, chagrined. "I didn't mean to—"

"No, stay," I say quickly. "I mean, if you want to—we should plan for the Bas Mitzvah Bash anyway."

"Right." Kayla smiles shyly at me again, her fingers running through her ponytail. I feel warmth like a little bubble in my chest. "I was thinking—what about a project of some kind? Maybe something we can make that we can bring home, like a charm bracelet or . . ."

"A charm bracelet would be cool," I say thoughtfully. "Mrs. Leibowitz, do you think the school would let us do that?"

Mrs. Leibowitz raises her eyebrows at us. "I think that if Beacon TDS has the budget for it, it might. But I can't imagine that it does." She perches onto her desk, contemplating. "There must be something out there that gets you excited."

"Pool parties," Kayla says, and she shoots me a conspiratorial grin. I grin back.

Mrs. Leibowitz sighs. "Anything else?" She pinches the bridge of her nose. "I'm trying to think of something too, but the only thing that's gotten you girls excited lately in class has been the guillotine." My eyes light up, and she stabs a finger at me. "*No.*"

"We liked the trebuchet too," Kayla says impishly. "I bet we could rig one of those up—"

Mrs. Leibowitz throws her hands up, smiling fondly at us. "You're going to get me fired," she says with an exaggerated sigh. "I know sixth graders love murder and mayhem, but there must be something a little more family friendly than *that*. Think. What interests you?"

I think of a door on the wall of the mikvah, of a secret passage that could lead anywhere. I think about laughing with Kayla in the mikvah and fighting the dybbuk while we wrestle with the showerhead. And when I look at Kayla, I know she's thinking about the exact same things as I am. "I don't know," she says.

Mrs. Leibowitz's phone buzzes, and she glances at it. "Think about it, okay, girls? I'm sure you'll come up with something." She grabs her phone and opens the door, leaving us alone in her office.

Kayla says abruptly, "You said the water isn't fully drained every day. How low does it go?"

"I've never watched it," I admit. "Ema usually does it in the morning while I'm at school." But I'm thinking now. "I bet we could figure out how to do it ourselves," I say. "It's just a drain. And there must be a way to pull it out and refill it. We'd have to wait until Ema's asleep because it'll take *forever* to fill up again. But we could lower the water enough that we could see what's in that door."

Kayla taps her fingers together. "We need to have a sleepover," she decides. "You and me, tonight. I have to figure out what's behind that door." She sees me staring at her, and she stares back. "What? Don't you want to find out?"

I blink at her, still startled. I have never, *ever* had a sleepover at my apartment before. And never in a million years would I have imagined having my first sleepover with Kayla. "Yeah," I say. "I do." Kayla tilts her head, expectant, and I say, "Kayla, would you like to sleep over tonight?"

Kayla beams. "I'd love to," she says.

Chapter 8

WE DON'T HAVE THE SLEEPOVER THURSDAY night, thankfully, because Ema never does get out of bed that day. It's a school night, and Mrs. Eisenberger puts her foot down. Instead, Kayla comes over on Saturday night, just after Shabbos ends, and she brings her math homework with her. "Ema says I have to do homework tonight," she says, rolling her eyes. "She has this *ridiculous* idea that I'm going to be too tired tomorrow to get anything done."

"That is ridiculous," I agree loudly. Mrs. Eisenberger gives us an unamused look. She's talking quietly to Ema at the front door, both of them smiling a lot and hesitating as they speak. This time, Ema is wearing one of her nicer Shabbos dresses, a black dress with gold patterning that she doesn't wear very often, and she doesn't look nearly as plain next to Mrs. Eisenberger as she did last time. "We're going to sleep right now," I announce, and I pause at the staircase up to our apartment.

Again, I remember how small it is and how little it'll look compared to Kayla's house. I've never been inside the house Kayla moved into a few years ago, a cozy little ranch house on a cul-de-sac. My apartment isn't even big enough to be *cozy*.

I blush as I lead Kayla up the stairs. I can feel her eyes on my back, then around the little kitchen with a rickety table in the corner and no space for anything else. There is a slight musty smell rising up from the laundry room, and there are plates from Shabbos still dirty in the sink. "It's not much," I say quickly. "But we don't really need much. Mostly, we hang out in the mikvah anyway. And we have a really big backyard because of the shul—"

My cheeks must be bright red. "Anyway, let's just put everything down in my room," I say on my way there. It's small too. There's a tiny dresser cramped against the back corner, clothes poking up from the lip of each drawer, and I have a few old school pictures on the top of the dresser and a pile of books that Mrs. Leibowitz keeps lending me and I keep forgetting to read. The walls are a plain white color, and I haven't tacked up anything on them except for an old velvet art piece that I made last year. My bed takes up most of the room, and there is a chair next to it that I usually use as a nightstand. Today it's folded up to make space for the futon that Ema and I set up for Kayla.

Kayla looks at the futon and then my too-small dresser. "I wish I had my own room," she says enviously. "My sisters leave their stuff everywhere. And when Shira comes over, I have to sleep on the floor. This futon looks comfy." She flops down onto it.

I exhale, relieved. "It's a good one," I say. "When I was younger, I used to get nightmares, and I'd drag the futon out of the closet and set it up next to my mother's bed." I'm too old to bring the futon to Ema's room anymore, even if I miss it sometimes.

Kayla laughs. "I would just crawl into my mother's bed," she admits. "You're much more considerate."

"It wasn't considerate." I lower my voice, widening my eyes. "She's a *kicker.*" We giggle together, the tension I feel fading away, and I plop down on my bed. "Do you really want to do math homework? We have some time to kill before Ema's asleep anyway. I think some people are coming to the mikvah tonight."

A woman's visit to the mikvah is supposed to be a totally private event, but in a mikvah this small, there are no secrets. Mrs. Cohen and Mrs. Feigenbaum have both scheduled visits, a rare occurrence, and I have to be on extra alert for the dybbuk.

Kayla bobs her head. "Do you have any snacks?"

We don't. I blink around, embarrassed again. Ema orders a delivery from the supermarket every Thursday, but she didn't know Kayla would be coming tonight and we have just enough snacks for the next week of school. I pretend to look through half-empty cabinets, knowing that there's nothing there, when Kayla says, "Aha!"

She lifts up a bag of chocolate chips and a bag of marshmallows from the baking cabinet. "Let's put them in a bowl together," she says. "There's *nothing* better in the world than chocolate chips and mini marshmallows."

"Just keep them away from the dybbuk," I warn her. "His specialty is open food. I once left my cereal and milk in the waiting room, and he smeared it across all the chairs."

Kayla peers at the staircase. "Does he ever come upstairs?"

"He stays in the mikvah." I shrug. "I've never seen him make it all the way up the stairs. The farthest he'll go is the lawn outside. Sometimes the shul, but not very often. He's attached to the mikvah."

"My father——" Kayla pauses, a flash of guilt passing across her face. I motion impatiently. I don't like pity, but I like it even less when people are afraid to talk to me. "My father says that a dybbuk is a spirit that never finished what it needed to do in this world. So it stays around and tries to finish it. You can get rid of them by saying Kaddish." My father said that too, back when I was little. I wonder if our fathers were friends, back when Ema and Mrs. Eisenberger were too. I don't remember any of it.

I shake off silly thoughts, returning myself to the present. "Not my dybbuk." Kaddish is a part of the daily davening. I can hear it from the shul on Shabbos even from a distance, and if I can hear it, the dybbuk can too.

"We should try it," Kayla says, carrying the bowl of food downstairs. "Where's the dybbuk now?"

The dybbuk is lingering in the middle of the waiting room, the chairs overturned, and I snap an irritated warning at him and hurry to fix the chairs before the mikvah visitors arrive. Kayla helps me, leaving the bowl on the table, and I yelp out, "No!" just as the dybbuk moves toward the bowl.

He freezes, standing between me and Kayla, and he gives me that insufferable smirk. I can see right through him to Kayla behind him, looking at me in alarm, and I say, "Kayla, pick up the bowl."

Kayla picks up the bowl. The dybbuk swoops at me and cackles as I duck, hovering on the other side of the room. Kayla watches me warily. "He's right here, isn't he?"

I nod, pointing at him. "Right there."

Kayla shivers. "Creepy." She sits down, grabbing a handful of marshmallows, and sets her math homework down on the table. "It's like when you see a spider but then lose it. You know it's somewhere in the room, and it could be crawling right over your leg, but you can't find it."

The dybbuk laughs silently, crouching down so he's staring face-to-face at Kayla. She looks right through him, squinting down at her homework, and he drags translucent fingers over her paper and then bounces away. "Don't worry," I lie. "He isn't anywhere near you right now."

Kayla jolts, her voice high. "Are you sure? I think I just felt . . . it was like cold fingers on my neck," she says, swallowing.

The dybbuk is moving rapidly, faster than I can follow him with my eyes. "I think so," I say, dizzy with the movements. "Let's just . . . let's focus on math."

But Kayla doesn't want to focus on math anymore. "That door must have something to do with the dybbuk," she says thoughtfully. "Maybe it's his unfinished business." Her eyes widen. "Maybe he was never buried, and it's his *body* in there."

I stare at her, horrified. I never considered that. "There's no body!"

"How do you know?" Kayla challenges me. She lowers her voice. "What if we pull that door open and there's something inside of it? Or just . . . a *face*, staring up at us on the mikvah wall." I shudder. The dybbuk hovers, watching me intently, and I try my best not to imagine him as a rotting body. "This mikvah is, like, a hundred years old. Maybe someone once killed a little boy in the mikvah, and now—"

The front door opens, and we both scream. So does Mrs. Feigenbaum, who is spry enough to stay upright but looks as though she might topple over from the force of two girls screaming at the top of their lungs at her. I hurry forward, catching her as she leans on the silver head of her metallic-blue cane. "Sorry! Sorry!"

Ema emerges from one of the bathrooms, bewildered as she glances between us. "What is going on out here?"

"Nothing!" I say hastily.

Mrs. Feigenbaum squeezes my shoulder. She smiles, her eyes nearly vanishing beneath the craggy wrinkles on her face. "It must have been that dybbuk of yours," she says, her fingers digging into my skin. I bob my head. It isn't *exactly* true, but it isn't *untrue* either. "Not to worry. I've been a little on edge myself. Especially after Wednesday morning . . ."

Ema's eyes round in concern. "How is your husband doing?" she asks gently. "I know that it must have—that you're both survivors—"

"Pach." Mrs. Feigenbaum swats at the air. "We are a nation of survivors. No one person holds ownership over *that*. How are you, mamaleh?"

Ema smiles, but it's brittle, just as stiff as it was after Wednesday morning's incident. "It was just a few lines in cement," she says. "Nothing to worry about. Now, why don't I get you set up with a bath?"

"You go to the *mikvah*?" Kayla blurts out. She's been watching us avidly, Mrs. Feigenbaum leaning on her cane and talking to Ema as though she's a little girl.

Mrs. Feigenbaum tuts with disapproval. "Are you calling me old, zeeskeit?"

Kayla flounders, at a loss for words. "N-no, ma'am," she says hurriedly. "You just . . . you look so *young*. I didn't realize you were old enough to go to the mikvah—"

Mrs. Feigenbaum nods gravely. "A common mistake," she says, a twinkle in her eye, and Kayla seems to relax. She waves at her bent, frail body, the gray strands of hair flying from her headscarf. "I know you wouldn't believe it from my youthful skin, but I'm older than I seem. I just moisturize."

"Amazing," Kayla says, nodding vigorously. "I want to age like you." She manages a straight face until Mrs. Feigenbaum turns, at which point she mouths, *Really?* at me. I shrug, grinning. Mrs. Feigenbaum is an acquired taste, but Kayla does okay.

The dybbuk hovers, waiting as Ema helps Mrs. Feigenbaum to one of the rooms. "Oh, you remind me of my little Shaindel," Mrs. Feigenbaum sighs, leaning heavily on Ema. "I admit, I might be a bit beyond the mikvah, but it was so important to me for so long . . ." She looks around our little room for a moment, nostalgic. "There was a time when this was the only mikvah that Beacon had, and all the women would crowd in here for appointments. Then they turned it into a Shabbos mikvah only." She smiles at Ema, whose returning smile looks a little strained. "I was so pleased when it was reopened for weeknights."

"Come with me," Ema says gently. "I'll bring you to your room."

She leads Mrs. Feigenbaum to the main bathroom, with its special rail for the handicapped, and we return to math just in time for another knock at the door. "Mrs. Cohen," I say, pulling the door open myself this time.

"Kohn? Cohn? No, I'm Mrs. Cohen," Mrs. Cohen corrects me. She's no-nonsense and a little odd, and I never get her jokes, but I try to laugh anyway. "Ah, Miss Eisenberger," she greets Kayla. "I haven't seen you at my Shabbos table in a while."

"Meira hasn't invited me in a while," Kayla says. Everyone in Beacon knows everyone else.

The dybbuk lurks, watching Mrs. Cohen speculatively, and I breathe a sigh of relief when Ema emerges from Mrs. Feigenbaum's bathroom to show Mrs. Cohen to hers. "He won't go in there when a woman is in there," I explain to Kayla. "It's immodest."

"I wonder if he'll try to stop us later," Kayla says thoughtfully. I poke her, but I wonder the same thing. The dybbuk lurks over us, watching and waiting. Somehow, I'm sure he knows exactly what we're planning.

Chapter 9

EMA GOES TO BED SOON AFTER Mrs. COHEN departs, leaving behind a fifty-dollar bill in the tip jar that Ema just stares at, at a loss. "I'll clean the bathrooms in the morning," she says finally, pocketing the money. "Aviva, remind me tomorrow to order new stockings for you."

I wiggle my toes, letting my big toe pop out of the rip in my current stockings. "Okay," I say dutifully. "Do you want me to run the dryer?"

Ema gives me a quiet, special smile, one shared silently between us. "No," she murmurs. "Enjoy your sleepover." She gives Kayla a smile of her own, then ducks down to kiss my forehead. "Come upstairs soon," she says. "I've already locked up."

We do go upstairs, making noise as we change into pajamas and listen for Ema. I can hear her even breathing, the quiet cadence as she sleeps, and we steal downstairs carefully, tiptoeing so the floorboards don't creak.

Kayla has brought along a bathing suit under her pajamas, and I've put on my own. We don't know how low we're going to be able to bring the water, and we might have to yank the door in the wall open against the water pressure and swim inside. Hopefully not.

"So there's some kind of lever or chain that pulls the drain out of the wall," I say in a whisper, leading Kayla into the mikvah. The dybbuk is lying in the bathtub in the spare bathroom, eyes half-closed as though he's sleeping, and I toss him a dubious look. He smiles, eyes lidded. "It'll take some time before enough drains out for us to get into the wall. We don't even know if the door's going to open."

"I wonder what we'll find down there," Kayla says, eyeing the still waters of the mikvah. "Something terrifying, I bet."

I give her a look and she laughs, smug in her recklessness. "Well, I *hope* anyway." She sits at the edge of the mikvah as I circle it, searching for a chain. "See? Mrs. Leibowitz was right. There is something else that interests me."

"Haunted mikvahs?" I spot the chain at last, poking out of the opposite corner of the mikvah, just beyond the staircase. "Bodies in the wall?"

"A dybbuk would make the Bas Mitzvah Bash better than what they have planned," Kayla says, rolling her eyes.

It feels a little like another jab, and I frown. "It's not *my* fault. And it's not like you don't *have* a mother—"

"Yeah, well, I wanted my father to come," Kayla snaps. It's sharp, a little mean again, and I can feel myself getting angry.

"So it's one less thing to do with your father," I burst out, frustrated. "So you'll go to the arcade together another time. Why does it *matter*? Why are you acting like it's the end of the world—"

I slip on the wet tiles, smacking my chin against the wall above the mikvah. Kayla is beside me in a moment, steadying me, helping me yank the chain.

With a great *whoosh*, the panel in the wall that plugs the drain is removed. I sink to the top step of the mikvah, staring sightlessly at the water as it begins to empty out into the basin belowground.

Kayla sits beside me, and she looks at me for a moment as though she's debating saying something. It's an expression I haven't seen in a long time, not since we were in second grade. Back then I sat with Kayla and never knew what to say to be her friend again. She didn't say the things we needed then either, but now she says quietly, "My father's sick."

I stare at her, surprised.

"He's been sick for a long time. We're not going to the arcade another time."

I don't know what to say to that, not beyond, "I didn't know." I've never heard a word of it from her or any of the other girls, even Shira, who can be a loudmouth. Kayla seems to have the perfect life most of the time, with all her siblings and her imposing mother and her friends and her top grades, and I've never seen any hint from her that she's been secretly suffering.

"No one knows," Kayla says, and she plays with the edges of her orange ponytail. "My family—we're not like *you*. We don't just tell people we're in trouble and hope that the community bails us out." It's angry, and it stings. Ema and I do everything we can to *avoid* people's charity, to keep on going in our quiet lives together where we don't need anyone else.

"That's not what we did," I retort, frustrated again. "And *we* would have helped you, if you hadn't just stopped *talking to me*—"

"Well, what was I going to say? My father is sick?" Kayla demands. She laughs sardonically. "Your father is *dead*. How was I supposed to complain to you about—about treatments and when it looked like he might be okay and when he relapsed—" Now she's crying, tears slipping down her cheeks into the mikvah, and I don't know what to say. "How was I supposed to talk to you at all?"

"You could have *tried*." A thought occurs to me, a realization that hurts my heart. "That's why your mother stopped trying with Ema too."

Kayla stares at the mikvah, face blotchy with tears. "We don't talk about it. Any of us. My Abba goes to shul and I *know* people see how he looks sometimes and whisper about it, but no one's brave enough to ask—"

"Well, your mother *is* kind of scary," I say, and Kayla laughs through her tears. I whisper, "I'm sorry. I wish—I wish you could still bring your father to the Bash. Maybe we could talk to Principal Axelrod about it—"

"She knows. She probably thinks she's doing me a favor too," Kayla says dully. "That they switched it for both of us. But if Abba was feeling well, I know he would have come. I *know* it." She doesn't sound very certain, and she looks relieved when she looks at the mikvah. "Hey," she says. "That was fast."

I blink at it. The water *has* drained quickly. It's nearly at the bottom step now, and the door in the wall is completely uncovered. We won't need our bathing suits, after all. "It's a big drain," I say, loosening the chain I'm still clutching in my hand. The drain is covered again.

I stand up, resting on the wall handle that I know will refill the mikvah again once we twist it. "Let's go," I say, pulling my pajamas up to my knees. Kayla hitches up her nightgown, crossing the shallow pool to the door.

She pries her fingers into the side of it, and the door slides open easily. "Whoa," Kayla says, peering inside.

"What?"

"There's a dead body in here." But she's grinning.

I elbow her, tilting my head to see inside. "Liar. Can you see anything?"

"We need a flashlight." We find one in Ema's closet in the back of the mikvah room. I hold on to the flashlight, shining it into the darkness.

Inside, there's just a dark passageway. I climb into it first, shuddering at the cold floor against my bare feet, and I sweep the flashlight around. "That's the draining pool," I say, my voice echoing through the passageway. "They must have dug this tunnel when they built the mikvah."

Kayla follows me in, looking where I'm pointing. There's a huge concrete wall in front of us, reaching up to the top of our passageway and down below it. "Is that it?" she says, disappointed. "I thought this was—wait." She turns, pointing behind me. "If this is just from the mikvah's construction, then why does it keep going?"

I swing the flashlight around again. This time, I catch a long passageway behind us, stretching out in the opposite direction of the door. "Where does it go?" I wonder, feeling a prickle of excitement.

"See, *this* is the stuff that would get me enthusiastic about the Bas Mitzvah Bash," Kayla says crossly. "Hauntings! Mysteries!

Something fun to do that isn't just us playing at a *Wheel of Fortune* machine for a few hours and dancing."

"So why can't we do that?" I say, and Kayla turns to me, her eyes wide.

"What do you mean?"

"I don't know." I'm thinking aloud. "Why can't we make it some kind of mystery? Like a scavenger hunt through the arcade. Or some kind of murder mystery."

"Or a scavenger hunt in the *dark*," Kayla says, and her eyes gleam with excitement. "Like this, but in groups. We could *do* that. And there are so many places to hide things in an arcade. We could even have a 'dybbuk' in each group whose job would be to secretly sabotage things."

I look around. Speaking of which, my dybbuk has been suspiciously calm since we came down here. He didn't even followed us into the mikvah room, and it has me suddenly wary.

I take a few quick steps forward, back to the door in the wall, and I see what we missed in our excitement.

The handle that feeds more water into the mikvah has already been turned, and the dybbuk is smirking at me from the opening in the wall. Water is leaking into the passageway already, draining into here instead of into the pool. "Dybbuk!" I say, furious, and I push at the door. "We have to get out of here—"

But the door won't move. Instead, it inches closer to me, the water pressure pushing it closed instead of open. "Kayla! Help me!" But the more we push, the more it seems to close.

"It won't open! We have to get in another way," Kayla says breathlessly.

"What way?" I demand. Even if we make it back aboveground somehow, the doors are double locked, and there are no windows on the ground floor of the mikvah. Wherever the passageway leads, it isn't going to take us back inside.

We're stuck. And meanwhile, the mikvah is filling up, unsupervised and unstoppable, and Ema doesn't have a clue.

Chapter 10

THE PASSAGEWAY IS SO DARK IT seems to swallow up the light I shine into it, but we trudge along, our bare feet making slapping noises against the rocky bottom of it. The dybbuk has joined us as we walk, his ghostly figure barely visible in the dark, but I refuse to talk to him. He's the one who got us into this mess.

Kayla holds my hand tightly. "Where are we?" she whispers. "Do you think this stretches out under the whole town?"

"I think we're under the shul," I whisper back. "We haven't been walking for that long." The cavern is cold and dark, but it winds with purpose, taking us down a careful route. There are no forks in the road, no other path to go on, and we keep a steady pace.

The cavern narrows more, and Kayla says in a hushed voice, "This must be how your dybbuk goes into the shul. Is it still with us?"

"Right next to me," I say, gesturing with my flashlight hand. The dybbuk moves peacefully through the cavern, bobbing along, and I toss him another dark glare. "I guess that's a good sign."

"I hope so." Kayla chews on her lip. "My mother's never going to let me come over again if she finds out what I've been doing here. She was nervous about me sleeping over after the swastika. . . ." She lets the sentence trail.

"It was just angry teenagers," I say. That's what everyone's been saying in school too. New Beacon has been really Jewish since it was developed. Beacon has become a busy hub for lots of younger families in the past decade, but not everyone has been happy about it.

Or so Mrs. Kohn said during her last visit to the mikvah. She didn't sound so sure that it was angry teenagers.

I shiver. "Why did your mother let you come, then?" I ask.

Kayla shrugs. "She likes your mother," she says. "And she likes you." I look at her, surprised. Kayla gives me a small smile. "I like you too, some of the time."

"Well, I like you some of the time too," I retort, but I can't quite stop myself from beaming. I turn away, toward the dybbuk, so Kayla can't see the stupid smile on my face. "Sometimes you're unbearable."

"Yeah?" Kayla says, her voice playful. "Well, sometimes, you're—genizah."

A genizah is a storage place for old holy books, before they're buried in the cemetery. I blink at her. "Is that supposed to insult me?"

"No," Kayla says impatiently. "That's where we are. Look." She points ahead, and I shine my flashlight in front of us as she tugs my hand. Up ahead, I see what she's seen—a window in a door, looming in front of us. And books.

Books. Dozens and dozens of old siddurim and other holy books, old and ripped up and stacked in piles just inside the door.

Stacks of loose papers with Hebrew writing, all wrapped and tied to keep them from flying away. We're in the shul's basement, right outside the genizah.

"That door had better open," I mutter, and Kayla runs ahead of me, wet feet slapping against the floor, and tries the doorknob. It opens. "Thank *god.*"

The dybbuk doesn't follow us into the genizah, and I take some satisfaction in closing the door on him. He watches me from the window, looking suddenly melancholy, and I turn away. "Now, we have to figure out how to get back into the mikvah before it floods the whole floor."

"There's a staircase." Kayla leads the way, letting me shine the flashlight ahead of us. We climb the stairs carefully, pushing open the basement door to stare at the shul in front of us. We're in the women's section, a carpeted area with a long dividing curtain across the side of it, and Kayla sits down heavily in one of the seats. "I am *exhausted,*" she proclaims, but she's grinning. "That was such a *rush.*"

"It's not over yet," I say grimly. "We still have to get back inside somehow and shut off the faucet." We could have slept in the shul overnight, I guess, and told Ema we got locked out by accident. But we have an hour or two before the faucet fills up the entire mikvah again. Ema has told me it can take up to three hours when the mikvah is totally empty.

"How are we going to get in?" Kayla wonders. "Is there a window we can climb out of into your apartment?" But the ceiling of the shul is high, far above us, and any helpful windows are way out of reach. There are tall stained-glass windows that begin lower down, but they don't open. "How about a key to the mikvah in the shul?"

"There must be one," I say, contemplating. "Just in case there's an emergency immersion and we're not home." The odds of Ema not being home are low, but *still*. "Let's check the rabbi's lectern."

We steal across the dark shul, weaving between the benches. There's an odd stillness to a shul at night, like a room frozen in an instant. I'm used to the shul being crowded on Shabbos, to weaving through rows of black-clad men wearing their white talleisim over their heads on a quest to find the candy man.

There is always a song to a shul, even when davening is over and people are using the room to study. A murmur of Hebrew, of words that feel ancient and sacred at once. People swaying, back and forth and back and forth. The shul is never silent, never still, and I shiver as I walk through the men's section toward the rabbi's table.

There is a cabinet beside it, and I see the lock on it and groan. "It's locked."

Kayla yanks at the lock and shakes it a few times. "It's loose," she corrects me, shaking it more violently. "Just a few more—"

"Who's there?"

We freeze. Another light sweeps over the room—someone else's flashlight, a man's voice coming closer. "Who's there?" he barks out, his voice sharp. "Come out *now!*"

We have no choice. Kayla drops the lock. Slowly, carefully, we tiptoe away from the corner by the cabinet, into the aisle at the center of the men's section. I can only imagine how we look, two girls in pajamas and bare feet in the middle of the shul, and I gulp.

A man comes into view, shining his flashlight at us, and I finally recognize him. It's the shammas, tasked as caretaker of the shul. He's about as old as Ema is, a tall man with dark hair under his yarmulke, and he squints at us suspiciously. "What are you two doing in the shul?" he demands.

"We were just—we got lost," I say lamely. Kayla bobs her head, eyes wide and afraid. I try to look as small and pathetic as possible. Maybe, if he feels bad enough, the shammas won't tell Ema he found me here. "We were locked out of my apartment. I thought the rabbi might have the key."

He peers at me. "You're the Jacobs girl," he says. "You shouldn't be wandering around at night." But his eyes soften, and he fiddles with a keychain he pulls from his pocket. "I have a key to the mikvah in here," he says, and Kayla and I exhale as one. "I don't have one to get into your apartment, though—"

"It's open," I say. "We just—we need to get back into the mikvah."

"I can do that," the shammas says, but he gives us a stern look as he turns to the door. "Be careful outside," he says. "You know better than anyone that these aren't days to be wandering the streets. It gives some people ideas."

He says it darkly, and I want to say, *I thought the symbol was just angry teenagers*, but I don't. I just watch him, my heart beating very quickly, and I don't say anything. Old memories tickle at the edges of my thoughts, struggling to break in, and I push them out before I get lost in them.

The shammas leads us down the steps to the grass, and I freeze on the steps. I don't know why. Something overwhelms me as though I can't move, as though I *have* to sit down and keep a vigil for something that's long over. I sink to the stairs, and Kayla says, "Aviva?"

She sounds frightened. "Ms. Jacobs," the shammas prods. I barely hear them. My eyes are lingering on the street, searching for something I can't even name. There is still a police car parked in front, and when I blink, I can see an echo of another, of figures moving on the lawn, of—

Of the dybbuk, crouched in front of me, nearly translucent in the moonlight. I jerk. I'm sitting on the steps, Kayla and the shammas just beyond the dybbuk, and I don't know how I've gotten here. I stand unsteadily. "Just hurt my foot for a second," I lie. "I'm fine."

We walk across the grass to the side of the shul, the stone path that takes us back to the mikvah, and Kayla thanks the shammas while I watch him unlock the door. He sighs, jabbing a finger at me. "Don't do this again. Next time, I tell your mother."

I watch him, an odd chill running through me as we depart. Kayla leads the way into the mikvah, which is only half full even now, and I sit numbly beside her as we watch the mikvah fill. "You're quiet," Kayla says, and she looks anxious, unnerved by my daze.

I struggle to put into words the strange distance I'm feeling. "It's just . . . my father used to be the shul shammas," I say finally. I remember him stacking books and straightening out benches after davening, and I remember dancing through the empty aisles of the women's section on Friday nights while the men sang on the other side of the curtain. I remember the shul being our domain, long before Ema and I moved into the tiny mikvah beside it.

Now, there is another shammas, another kind man who looks after the shul. I don't know how to feel. There's an aching cavern in my heart, an Abba-shaped hole that feels like it's going to be there forever. I try not to think about it. It's been almost five years, and I do okay when I cover it up and pretend I'm fine. I *have* to cover it up because five years is so long to spend with a shadow over my heart, and I don't know how to go out into the world if I leave it uncovered. I'd be like Ema, alone in a house with a bunch of big brown delivery boxes the only evidence there's a world outside.

But today, seeing another shammas with those keys jangling from his hand, that cavern feels huge and inescapable, like a black hole that will swallow up the rest of me if I stay in it for much longer.

"Oh," Kayla whispers.

Her hand slips into mine, and I feel its warmth through the chill that seems to envelop my body.

Chapter 11

"It'd be kind of like a scavenger hunt," Kayla explains. "But with dybbuks. We're going to use Jell-O."

"Jell-O," Principal Axelrod says slowly, as though she doesn't quite follow. "How will the Jell-O help the scavenger hunt?"

I pick up Kayla's thread. "We're going to make individual Jell-O cups. Each group is going to get a set of cups with their first clue inside the Jell-O. But one person in each group of cups is also going to get one with a mark on it that means they're the dybbuk."

"And the dybbuk is there to sabotage the group. Give them bad advice, work against them—it's the dybbuk's job to stop the group from making it to the end. And no one knows who the dybbuk is," Kayla explains eagerly. "The clues can be taped to games or might even be inside the game, if the arcade will work with us. We have a lot of ideas."

Principal Axelrod contemplates. "We could arrange a prize for the winning team," she says slowly. "I think we'd have space in the budget for something substantive."

Kayla and I exchange glances, astonished. "Does that mean we can do it?" I say. I didn't really believe Principal Axelrod might *agree* to it. It's a grand plan, one that lets us completely restructure the Bas Mitzvah Bash.

Principal Axelrod's eyes twinkle. "Ordinarily, I might have my doubts," she says. "But I haven't seen you two agree on anything in years, let alone be this excited for it. I think this will be a lot of fun for your grade. They're lucky to have you."

"Thank you!" I keep saying when we leave Principal Axelrod's office. "Thank you! We're going to do this well, I promise!"

It's been a week since we first met with Principal Axelrod, and the Bas Mitzvah Bash is only two weeks away now. Kayla and I spent the week fine-tuning the idea we had in the mikvah, figuring out what kinds of clues we might use and how we'd work the start of the scavenger hunt.

It was Ema's idea to use Jell-O, and she's been more animated than I've seen her in a while, searching online for the perfect recipe and little cups for them. Kayla has spent most nights this week at the mikvah with us, planning in between the rare visitor. The three of us have been working out different clues, putting them together and making them into rhyming couplets.

We've even been talking in school now, glued together like we were back in second grade. "We have *so* much to do," Kayla says as we exit the office, ticking off each point on her fingers. "First, we have to talk to the arcade and see if they'll let us come in early to set up."

"I really love the idea of having some of the clues as high scores," I say, thinking. It's probably not possible, not without us spending the whole day at the arcade beforehand *setting* those high scores, but it's nice to imagine it. "Or of hiding one inside of a bowling ball."

"Yes! And we can have workers there holding a few too. We can do this," Kayla says happily. "Oh! My mother suggested that we go to the arcade on Sunday with her to see where we want to put the clues. Are you in?"

I haven't been to the arcade since my family used to go together during Pesach vacation, all three of us. I was too little to do much, but there's a ball pit in one of the side rooms and a whole section filled with bouncy houses, and I remember jumping through both with Abba and Ema waiting on the side, laughing and cheering me on.

It feels like another lifetime when I think back to it. "Yeah! If you're sure. I know we've spent a lot of time on this already—"

Kayla shrugs. "It's been fun." She tosses me a grin. "And it's *working*. Everyone I tell about it has been super excited about the Bash. People like *doing* things, not just hanging out at an arcade playing games." She makes a face. "The only part of this I'm not into is not getting to be one of the people doing the scavenger hunt. I'd make a mean dybbuk."

"Please," I scoff. "I'd be the best dybbuk in our group. I know exactly what a dybbuk would do."

"I'm learning!" Kayla says brightly. "The dybbuk threw my homework in the mikvah last time I was over, so I feel like I'm pretty much part of the family now." We both laugh. We were lucky that it was Kayla's history homework because Mrs. Leibowitz knows about the dybbuk. She just sighed and gave Kayla an extension. "Anyway, we could have been in rival groups. I'd have *won*."

"Not against me," I say, very sure that I'd have been the winner. "We'll never know, though. We're making up all the clues. It wouldn't be fair."

"I know, I know," Kayla sighs as we round the corner back to the sixth grade hallway. "I do like running things, though. We really are good at this—" She stops, frowning. "What's going on?"

The hallway is crowded for lunchtime, more so than usual, and we press forward to see what's going on. Everyone is gathered around the sixth grade bulletin board, pressing in close. "Yes!" shouts someone. It's Esther, and I bite my lip as I finally figure out what everyone's trying to see.

Esther breaks from the crowd, her pale face flushed with victory, and she bellows, "I made it!" Two of her friends wrap their arms around her, spinning with her in delight. Kayla reaches for my hand. I squeeze hers.

Esther catches sight of us, and her smile fades from her face. "I made it," she says, much more apologetic. She plays with the waist of her skirt. "I don't know if I would have if you two had been in the running."

"You're a good player," I say. I try to be as gracious as I can, even though I kind of want to throw a tantrum right now. "Who else was on the machanayim list?"

"Chaya Leah, Maryam, and Shira. A good showing," Esther says. "Two girls from our class and one each from the others. We're just alternates—we probably won't even get to play—" She stumbles over the words, but she can't quite shake the sheer excitement in her eyes. "It's not a big deal."

"It is a big deal," Kayla says. She's also trying to be gracious, but I can hear the edge in her voice. "Mazal tov. I hope you get a chance to play."

The smile finally spreads across Esther's face. "Me *too*," she says, and she beams and bounces away with her friends.

"Lucky," I mutter, my excitement for the Bash replaced with glumness.

"It's fine," Kayla says, bumping my shoulder with hers. Her skin is warm beneath her polo, and her hair smells faintly of coconut, like it always did when we were younger. "We'd be too busy for practice anyway. The machanayim game is on the day after the Bas Mitzvah Bash."

"Yeah," I say wistfully. "I'd probably be too nervous for the game to enjoy myself at the Bash, then. Poor Esther."

"Poor Esther," Kayla echoes, sounding equally unconvinced. The crowd is beginning to dissipate as the names get out, and we're offered many, many pitying looks. It should have been us, and everyone knows it. But there's nothing we can do about it now.

I glance at my watch, a silvery analog one Ema ordered for me last Chanukah. "You know," I say, looking around at the hallway and the buzz of excitement for something we can't be a part of, "we still have another ten minutes to lunch."

Kayla's eyes clear. "Let's go upstairs," she says.

The roof is all but empty, a lone teacher supervising a gaggle of eighth graders at the other end, and Kayla picks up a machanayim ball and throws it at me. I catch it easily, firing it back at her with equal force. "We'll make the team next year," I decide. "Together. Then in eighth grade, one of us will be the captain."

It's a nice thought, being teammates with Kayla. Being *friends* with Kayla beyond the Bas Mitzvah Bash. I try to imagine the future, playing together and finally taking down our rival school, and I catch Kayla's next ball with extra energy.

"You know it," Kayla says fiercely. "We're going to win two years in a row. No one stands a chance against us." She catches the ball and sends it back to me. I snatch it from the air, preparing to throw it back.

"Us?" a voice repeats from behind us, and my throw goes high, up between us so Kayla has to jump to catch it. Shira is standing next to the door on the roof, her hands on her hips. "What's *with* you, Kayla?" Shira demands. "You've been obsessed with Aviva all week."

She looks hurt and a little angry, her nose even more pinched than usual. "Next thing you know, you're going to run around shouting about ghosts all day," she says spitefully, glaring at me.

Kayla looks pained. "Shira," she says, and I remember that they're best friends. Until a week ago, Kayla and Shira were inseparable. Shira looks at me like I'm the enemy, like I'm the only one keeping Kayla from her, and I clench my jaw, ready for whatever she might snap at me. Kayla says, "It's not a ghost. It's a dybbuk."

"No, it's a *joke*." Shira sneers. "Another made-up story so Aviva can get some more of the attention she desperately wants."

She circles us for a moment, and I twist around, defensive. "Oh, and is that better than you following Kayla around, hoping for her attention?" I snap. "There *is* a dybbuk at the mikvah—"

Shira laughs. "*Please*," she says. "There's barely even a mikvah."

Stung, I drop the ball. "What's that supposed to mean?"

"That mikvah wasn't even *open* until your mother needed a *job*," Shira spits out. "I've heard my sisters talking." Shira has six older sisters, and four of them are married. None go to our mikvah, not like Shira's aunt, Mrs. Blumstein of the pretty sloped face. "It's just charity because she wouldn't accept anything else. Everyone knows it."

I stare at her. "That's not true," I say coldly. "The mikvah was reopened because Beacon is getting bigger. That's all."

"Yeah?" Shira challenges. "How many women do you get a night? My sisters say the New Beacon Mikvah is always packed." I don't answer. She smirks, satisfied. "My aunt only goes to your mikvah because she feels sorry for you and your shut-in mother—"

It's Kayla who moves before I can, stepping between us with her eyes dark and narrowed. "Stop it, Shira," she says, her voice like steel. "Go *away*."

Shira bursts into tears. "Why do you even *like* her?" she demands. "You hated her for so many years! What does Aviva have that I don't—"

Kayla looks very lost. Suddenly, I don't want to be there anymore. I walk away from Kayla and Shira, off to the corner of the roof, and I stare past the fence at the street down below.

Shira's *wrong*, except I know she isn't. She's just said things I've known deep down for a while. Ema and I are managing, just barely, but we shouldn't be managing at all. We were barely managing back when Abba was alive and Ema was working full-time as a teacher. The mikvah mysteriously needed a caretaker just after Ema quit her job as a teacher, just after the New Beacon mikvah expanded. The mikvah came with an apartment, free of charge, and I never questioned it. I never even questioned Mrs. Feigenbaum's visits or the large tips each of our visitors bring.

But it's all charity, of course, the community quietly providing tzedakah for a girl and her—her *pathetic* mother, who *is* a shut-in and an outcast and who can't even go outside to buy food for Shabbos. I blink away tears, forcing those thoughts from my mind. Ema is the strongest person I know. She's survived so much, all on her own, and anyone who thinks like Shira doesn't deserve to know her. Ema tries *so hard*, and I'm just—I just—

I'm crying just as hard as Shira is sobbing across the roof, and I turn away so Kayla can't see me, clenching my fists and staring desperately out at the blue-gray roofs of the houses lined up in a row below us, each one neat and perfect in its place. The trees shade backyards full of toys and garnished with swing sets, bikes discarded at doors in a perpetual sign of *life*, of a world that feels so distant from my own. I don't know why I'm crying—if I'm sad or guilty or just mad—and I don't know if I'm crying for myself or for my mother or for all the words I just thought about Ema, who doesn't deserve a single one of them.

Pach, Mrs. Feigenbaum spat during her last visit to the mikvah. *We are a nation of survivors.* Ema survives, and that matters so much more than Shira will understand, and somehow that makes me cry even harder.

Chapter 12

THE SHUL IS BRIGHT WITH LIGHT and color and song during Shabbos, a peace settling over it that I like even when I'm in the women's section. I come almost every Shabbos morning, even though none of my classmates do. It's mostly older women and little kids scrambling back and forth between the men's section and ours, proudly proffering lollipops and candy after each trip. The sun hits the stained-glass windows just right during the morning, refracting reds and blues and greens across seats and onto the rich maroon curtains that separate the two sections, and the whisper of dresses as they swish against cushioned seats is like an echo of the whispers of davening around me. When the men sing, their davening like a reverberating chorus throughout the shul, some women sing along, their high voices weaving beautifully into the fabric of the song.

I like the energy of it, the way I can close my eyes and recite davening under my breath and feel like I'm a part of something much bigger than myself. Without school to escape to on weekends, the mikvah is too cramped, too lonely, the walls pressing in on me. I go out to the shul on Shabbos to be surrounded by people, by other girls and women with the same joined purpose as me.

Ema never comes, of course, and it bothers me today more than it has in a long time. Shira's words are still ringing through my head, and I blush and look around, my eyes drawn to the little girl who sits in the row in front of me. She has a stack of books next to her, and she leafs through them, eyes flickering from picture to picture while her mother prays.

At one page, she stops, and she tugs her mother's arm. Her mother sets down her siddur to beam at her daughter. The girl is excited about something on the page and her mother's eyes glow with the same enthusiasm, leaning down to whisper something in the girl's ear.

The cantor begins to sing the next part of the davening, his familiar voice not beautiful as much as it is steady and keeps the key, and the girl stands up on her wobbly chair, leaning against her mother to sing softly into her shoulder. I watch them swaying together, and I feel sick.

I don't know why. It isn't like watching my classmates with their fathers. I don't have Abba anymore, but Esther's or Shira's or Hodaya's fathers aren't *mine*, and it hurts but in a different way. I still have Ema. I remember going to shul with her when I was little, just like that girl, and I remember whispered secrets and my high, squeaky voice singing along with the davening.

I haven't thought of Ema as someone I've *lost*, not until now, steaming from Shira's words two days ago and watching another little girl with her mother. My eyes sting, and I press my siddur to my face to hide as I blink rapidly.

Around me, I can hear singing, and I keep my face in my siddur, hands pressed to its covers, swaying to the song as I fight tears. I don't like to cry. Sometimes it feels like if I start, I'll never stop crying. I don't want to be like that—*like Ema*, that nasty voice in my head says, and the tears finally fall free.

No, I think fiercely. *No, no, no.* Ema is strong, is fighting in her own way, and I have to stop letting Shira get to me. I'm strong too, because Ema needs me to be. Aviva Jacobs does *not* have a breakdown in the middle of the shul on Shabbos morning. Because we're fine.

My breathing is shallow, my heart racing in my chest, and I don't know if I'm shaking or swaying anymore. The final song of davening is coming to a close, and I can hear people walking around me, maneuvering past me to put their siddur away. I tremble, and I can feel tears, but I'm not crying. You have to be able to breathe to cry.

I try to gasp in air, but a terrible scraping sound comes from my throat instead. *I can't breathe*, I think, and now I'm beginning to panic. My heart feels as though it might beat right through my ribs, moving faster than I've ever felt it before, and my hands falter on the siddur—

I hear the rustle of the curtains that separate the men and women's sections of the shul, and the siddur is nudged from my hands. I choke, startled at the sudden surge of light filtering in without the siddur in front of me, and I catch sight of a boy in the women's section.

No. Not a boy. The dybbuk hovers in front of me, his eyes mischievous as though this is just another day at the mikvah. No one else has noticed us yet, me gasping in breaths that aren't reaching my lungs and him floating right in front of me. I can't let anyone see me. I can't—

The dybbuk sweeps his hand across the bookcase and sends a

row of siddurim tumbling to the ground. *"Dybbuk!"* I hiss, and he smirks unapologetically as I scramble to pick them up. Women turn at the commotion, and I look down swiftly, keeping my eyes on the ground as I kiss each one and stack them up into a pile. No one sees my red eyes or tearstained face.

I don't realize until I'm walking down the stairs from the shul and heading back to the mikvah that my breathing has returned to normal and I'm not crying anymore. I got distracted before I could get stuck in a black hole of emotion I can't climb out of, I guess. The dybbuk is good for *something*.

I toss him another sullen look as he watches me from the doorway to the shul. He doesn't come out on to the lawn with me, and I dawdle, unwilling to go back into my quiet little apartment just yet. Instead, I stare blankly out at the lawn, the sun filtering in through the trees and the little boys and girls running and shrieking across the low-cut green grass that stretches in a wide, thick rectangle in front of the shul and the mikvah tucked in beside it. Ema will be in the mikvah waiting room, praying in a corner and setting the table for our Shabbos meal, and it will feel too small for the two of us right now.

I know I can't leave the grounds of the shul without Ema panicking, so I wander up and down the lawn and listen to the chatter of the other congregants as they filter out of the shul, the rise and fall of small talk and laughter that comes after a few hours of simultaneous solitude and unity. There are more girls here now, come to pick up their parents or to go inside for a little bit of post-shul cake at the kiddush, and I spot Mrs. Blumstein walking out with a plate and two girls beside her.

I see Shira first, and I duck behind a stack of freshly delivered packages next to the mikvah door. Then I catch sight of a flash of copper hair and step back out. Kayla sees me right away, and she heads over to me, Shira following with reluctance. "Aviva!" she says brightly, holding out her plate. "Did you get potato kugel?"

I shake my head. "I'm not hungry," I say, suddenly self-conscious. Ema and I get the leftovers from the kiddush. I'll be having plenty of potato kugel then. "Hi."

"Hi." She beams at me. "Shira's staying at her aunt's house for Shabbos, and she picked me up for the meal." Shira is watching me with an icy look, and I glare back at her.

Mrs. Blumstein, her sensible black dress stained slightly on the skirt from what looks like fallen kugel, doesn't seem to notice. "Why don't you join us too, Aviva?" she says, smiling fondly at me.

It isn't *just* Shira's outraged glower that makes me want to come. Her words are still echoing through my mind, and I need to *breathe*, to be outside of the mikvah for a little while. I don't want to go back inside—I desperately want to be *out*, and I say, "I just need to ask my mother."

I push open the door to the mikvah a crack. Behind me, I can sense Shira shifting forward, craning her neck to see inside. My shoulders tighten. I don't want Shira to get any more ammunition to use against me.

But Kayla says, "Go ahead." It's a hopeful murmur, and I realize she *wants* me to come with them. I haven't been *wanted* in a really long time. It's a weird feeling.

I open the door all the way. Ema is standing in the corner, eyes closed tightly as she prays. She's wearing the ratty old robe she puts on every Shabbos. It was once a silky material, royal blue and so beautiful I thought she looked like a queen in it. It got dirty and ragged when she was in the ambulance, before Abba—

Now, it's loose around her, and it doesn't look beautiful or regal anymore. Our Shabbos table is set already, the coffee table covered in a stained white cloth and our chipped china set out on the table. Usually, I like the Shabbos meal, the quiet mood and Ema trying her hardest to sit opposite me at the table each week. But today, all I can see is how Shira must be seeing it. Like we're *pathetic.* Like Ema really is someone to pity.

Ema doesn't turn around, still immersed in her davening, and I imagine her putting away my plate and sitting down to eat the meal alone. *No.* She probably won't eat at all if I'm not here to sit with her.

When Ema does turn, she looks startled, then manages a smile. "Kayla," she says, looking warmly at the girls behind me in the doorway. "And . . . Shira?"

Shira bobs her head, her eyes darting toward me. I glower at her, challenging her to say something more to Ema, but she only ducks her head and refuses to look at either of us. Kayla says, "We wanted to invite—"

I can see Ema's face closing off, shadows falling upon it as her smile turns to fragile glass. She is nodding, but it looks like it's painful, like someone has stuck a hand on to her neck and is moving her head up and down with it.

"I can't go," I blurt out. Kayla looks at me in confusion. I bite my lip. "Sorry. I just realized that I have . . . a really bad stomachache."

"A stomachache?" Ema echoes worriedly, moving to me to press her hand against my forehead. "You *are* a little warm," she says. "It could be the stomach flu, or—" She stops, falling silent.

We all stand awkwardly in the little waiting room, avoiding each other's eyes, and it's Mrs. Blumstein who finally clears her throat to speak. "You're welcome to come over later if you're feeling better," she says kindly to me, and I barely manage a nod. Kayla still looks confused. Shira won't look at me at all.

I don't come over. Instead, I eat a quiet meal while Ema sits opposite me and doesn't speak. Her eyes are empty, her figure slumped in her too-big robe, and I am too old to be frightened by it. In a few hours, she'll be back to normal, and we'll play Scrabble on the floor and then stretch out on her bed and talk until she drifts off.

For now, I sit on a chair with my fingers wrapped around my glass and my mouth full of potato kugel and cholent, and I don't try to get through to Ema right now. My stomach *does* hurt now, and I try not to imagine the Blumstein house, alive with chatter and laughter and *normal* in a way my house hasn't been in five years.

The dybbuk sits beside me, dressed in a smart Shabbos suit and his olive-toned face glimmering with mischief. He looks as ordinary as any of the boys I saw leaving the shul today, his hair a little too shaggy at the front and his frame lanky and relaxed, and he eyes the potato kugel like he wouldn't mind eating it too. He tips over my glass every time I let go of it, and I watch him instead of Ema until the meal is over.

Chapter 13

EMA CONTEMPLATES THE WORDS ON HER screen. "How about this?" she says, typing for a moment.

> *A summer night, quiet delight, but wait!*
> *A big-jawed creature pops up from deep beneath the lake.*

Kayla peers at the screen. "Is that . . . the game where you bop the hippos?" she asks.

Ema nods smugly. "You can stick the next clue into the hippo's mouth," she suggests.

"Mrs. Jacobs, that's *brilliant*," Kayla says enthusiastically, marking it down on her checklist. We each made one, a list of every single hiding spot we found when we visited the arcade last Sunday. It's now just the night before the Bas Mitzvah Bash, and we're all hard at work.

Mrs. Eisenberger has even come with Kayla once or twice to help set up clues, but she doesn't have much time. She looks more haggard than usual, her clothing disconcertingly casual and her face free of makeup, and Ema makes her coffee and sits with her, murmuring in the kitchen. Mr. Eisenberger is having a bad month, and Kayla tells me she's been busy caring for him. Kayla's older siblings are busy with him too, and Kayla has thrown herself into the Bash planning.

We're making Jell-O while Ema works on new clues, pouring hot water, then cold, into bowls of differently colored Jell-O mixes. Carefully, I place a little piece of paper into each of the little cups Ema ordered online for us, then spoon out some Jell-O to harden around it.

"Hopefully, the Jell-O doesn't make the paper too damp to read," Kayla says, eyeing a collection of finished cups. We've made one batch just to test them out, and we'll be trying them tomorrow. They're supposed to sit in the fridge for a while before they solidify. The mix also warns us to keep them in the fridge until eating, so we're going to bring them downstairs.

The mikvah has its own fridge in the laundry room, a machine used so rarely Ema usually keeps it unplugged. Tonight, we've plugged it in, and Kayla and I are filling up trays of Jell-O to put inside of it. "Sixty-three girls and mothers makes about a hundred and thirty Jell-O cups," Kayla says, counting the ones we've already done. "Seven teams of eighteen members each. We've done . . . three teams so far."

"You should bring down the trays now," Ema suggests. "We're going to need the table space soon." The trays are crowded on the kitchen table, filling up nearly all the space we have, and Kayla and I each balance a tray in our hands.

I'm careful on the stairs, very aware of how narrow and shaky they are, but I don't plan for one thing—a sudden movement beneath me, the dybbuk shooting right up to greet me. The Jell-O flies out of my hands and I tumble down the stairs with a scream, plastic cups crashing onto me until I'm covered in multicolored Jell-O.

"Aviva!" Kayla calls, alarmed, and she sets her tray down at the top of the stairs and hurries to me. "Are you okay?"

"The dybbuk got me," I say irritably, brushing Jell-O off my cheeks. It's everywhere, red and green and yellow all over the stairs and the walls and my clothes. "You know, just once, I'd like to do *something* without you ruining it," I snap to my right, where I can feel the dybbuk hovering. "Is that too much to ask?"

The dybbuk only laughs at me, unapologetic, and that makes me even more annoyed, frustrated again at how nothing can *change*, how Ema can be animated and life can be kind of okay but there's still a dybbuk trying to sabotage us. "You know what?" I say, jabbing a finger at him. "That's enough. I'm going to *stop* you."

Kayla steps down beside me, squinting at what must be empty space to her. "How do we stop a dybbuk?"

"I don't know." I contemplate, remembering what she suggested before. I want the dybbuk *gone*, especially now that I'm doing things that *matter* and he's still trying to ruin everything. "Do you think Kaddish might really work?"

Kayla shrugs. "It's worth a try."

We take down the other two trays without any incidents, and I say to Ema, "Kayla and I are going next door for a minute, okay?"

Ema's face tightens. "It's just the shul," I promise. "I won't even leave our property. I just want to look something up. And I won't be alone."

"I can go with you," Ema offers finally. It takes something out of her just to say it, and I can see it on her face. It is difficult to turn her down, but I don't think she'll be happy with the idea of us battling the dybbuk.

"We'll be *fine*," I promise. "You can watch us go if you want. It'll just be a few minutes."

I know she's thinking about the symbol on the sidewalk when she hesitates, but I also know she's going to give in. Nothing else has happened since that symbol appeared. It was a one-time thing, just like all the other little incidents we whispered about afterward—kids getting harassed for their yarmulkes or people shouting insults from across the street. Beacon is *safe*, as long as you don't venture out too far on your own.

Ema sighs. "All right," she says. "I'll keep working on clues." She turns back to her laptop, eyes focused on the screen, and I swallow back my surprise and head downstairs to Kayla and the dybbuk. Ema is trying. It's my turn to try too.

"Come with me," I order the dybbuk. He crosses his eyes at me and wheels around in a circle, but he follows me outside to the lawn.

Kayla looks around warily. "Do you think it's safe out now?" I don't answer, glancing at the quiet street across the lawn from the shul. In the dark, I can see the shadows of the houses like black-gray shapes stretched along the street, and bikes and strollers have been tucked away for the evening. A few stray windows are lit up, the only sign of life on a sleepy block, and I see the figure of a familiar neighbor walk past one window and feel a little more secure. Then someone drives past, their headlights illuminating us for a moment, and we both freeze in the light and relax when the car goes on.

The dybbuk shifts, antsy, and I say, "Let's go inside." The shul is unlocked until the shammas comes to clean up and lock it at around midnight, so we still have a number of hours. Still, it's dark and empty, and I shiver as Kayla and I step inside.

The dybbuk circles the room, eyeing us warily. I refuse to meet his eyes. He's my worst enemy, but he's also been kind of a friend—my only friend for a long time—and I don't know how I feel about sending him away. But it's *enough* already. It'll be better for both of us if the dybbuk can move on to the next life.

Kayla takes a siddur from the shelf and opens it, walking over to the podium at the front of the men's section. The room is big and grand, rows and rows of cherry wood pews with lecterns in front of them, and the podium is in the center of the rows. Behind it is the ark, a cabinet with a velvet curtain in front of it embroidered with the Ten Commandments in Hebrew and with holy Torah scrolls inside.

I stand at the podium with Kayla, and Kayla whispers, "You should do it. It's your dybbuk."

I nod, swallowing. The dybbuk pauses in front of a stained-glass window decorated with the lion of Judah, the colors behind him painting his translucent body in a rainbow of light. He stares down at me, and I carefully read the tefillah for the deceased. "*Yisgadal v'Yiskadash Shemei Raba—*"

The dybbuk begins to understand what we're doing. He whirls around in a frenzy, circling the room faster and faster, just as he did when Kayla first suggested it. "Amen," Kayla whispers, the appropriate response.

I stumble over the next words, less familiar than the first, the ancient Aramaic a language I hardly know. Kayla and I say the next response together as the dybbuk's movements take on a new wildness, shooting up and down and over us as we recite the words together. *"Amen! Yehei shmei raba mevorach l'alam ul'almai almaya."*

The dybbuk hurls himself at me again, and this time, he's coming directly at me. I stumble back, slipping on the floor, and I can see the dybbuk's face twisted with rage and betrayal. *"Yisbarach v'yishtabach v'yispa'ar v'yisromam v'yisnasei,"* I gasp out, mostly from memory. The dybbuk isn't fading, isn't relieved, and I falter in the middle of the Kaddish. "I can't do this," I say finally, breathing hard. "I can't—he doesn't want it."

"He needs it," Kayla counters, peering around the room. But she can't see the horror on the dybbuk's face, the pain as I try to send him away.

"He doesn't," I say, my heart heavy. "It's hurting him. I'm hurting him." I pick up the siddur, and I can't meet Kayla's eyes. "I don't want to—I can't do this to him."

Kayla is studying me, biting her lip as though she wants to say something more, but she doesn't. "Okay," she says. "It's your dybbuk. You decide." She shrugs, waving it off as though nothing very big just transpired. "The dybbuk isn't all bad," she offers. "He got us to be friends again, didn't he?"

I smile. The dybbuk stops moving frantically, settling against my side for a moment, and then he soars away. "He looks out for me when he isn't trying to get me in trouble," I admit. "Speaking of which, we should get back to the apartment. Ema's going to *freak* if we don't come back soon."

We trudge back to the mikvah. I feel very silly about the whole thing, trying to send the dybbuk off just because he knocked over some Jell-O. We have more than enough Jell-O and more than enough cups. One mishap isn't that bad.

But the dybbuk is sulking at my attempt, missing when we finish up the Jell-O and carefully carry them to the fridge. He doesn't return while we put the finishing touches on the last few clues, while Ema prints them and Kayla cuts them out, while I settle on the floor of the mikvah waiting room and curl each slip of paper into a cup.

"I haven't seen the dybbuk since we got back from the shul," I whisper to Kayla when we finally get into bed.

She shrugs. "He'll turn up. He always does, right?" she says. "He's probably just mad at you."

"He's never mad at me. I'm the one who gets mad at *him*. I don't know what he'll do when he's mad," I say glumly. "I should—I'm going to go back to the shul. Make sure he found his way home. He wasn't with us when we walked out."

Kayla brightens. "He could have gone through the passageway," she reminds me. "Maybe he's hanging out in there. We know he likes it down there." She thinks hard. "We can go in from the other direction—from the genizah. That way we don't get stuck in the passageway."

We're quiet as we slip downstairs in our pajamas, this time with shoes on. I take the keys to the mikvah with me in my pocket. No mistakes this time. I don't want to have to see the shammas again.

It's just before midnight, and we don't have much time before the shammas arrives. Swiftly, we walk to the shul, pushing the doors open. "Dybbuk?" I call, peering around in the dimness. "Dybbuk, can you *please* just come home—"

Kayla gasps. The sound splits the silent room, and I see only then what she's already spotted.

In the hours since we were last here, the shul has been wrecked. *Destroyed*. The beautiful tapestry over the ark has been shredded, the pews overturned and broken, and one has been lifted and hurled into a stained-glass window. Siddurim are littered across the ground, a bookcase toppled over and nothing but broken pieces of wood. There is destruction everywhere I look: the shattered *ner tamid*, a light that's supposed to be eternal now black and dull, the rich maroon curtain between the men's and women's sections torn down and the shiny golden rod that held it buried in the podium.

Kayla lets out a pained cry, running across broken glass as she hurriedly reaches for the siddurim lying on the floor. She tries to pick them up, gathering them in her arms, and I say urgently, "Kayla, *no!*"

Kayla twists around to stare at me. "What do you mean, no? We can't leave these on the floor! They're siddurim!"

"The police are going to come," I say, and I feel numb. I know this part. I remember this part, even if everything before it is a blank space in my mind. I know police and flashing lights and my own face reflected in the tinted windows of a car, glowing red with the shul framed behind it. I can't feel anything when I think about it, not fear or rage or grief. If I feel too much, I think I'll just stop moving entirely. "We can't tamper with a crime scene. We can't—"

I lift my eyes. The dybbuk is perched at the top of a tall window, this one too high to be broken. His eyes are haunted, and I breathe, filled with horror and dread, "What did you do?"

He doesn't answer. He never does.

Chapter 14

It's a terrifying secret that Kayla and I hold together, one we can't tell anybody. I try to tell Ema, who I think is the only one who might understand. "The dybbuk did it—"

"Not now, Aviva," Ema whispers, and she holds me tightly as we sit on the steps up to the narrow stoop outside the mikvah door, watching the police as they enter and leave the shul. There are police lines everywhere and crowds of people—both Jewish and not—on the other side of the lines, craning to see. Ema and Kayla and I have front-row seats from the mikvah, police hurrying right past us as they search the perimeter of the shul. It is morning, and the sun shines down through gray clouds, the air damp and thick around us. Ema is wearing a dark, soft sweater that hangs off her frame, her grasp almost painful on my arm.

One of the police officers smiles kindly at us beneath a thick mustache. "We are taking this very seriously," he promises. "Vandalism has been fairly common in the neighborhood lately. I don't think we've seen enough to consider this a hate crime."

"What would be enough?" Ema says tightly. "A swastika on the sidewalk in front of the shul, maybe?" She sounds different.

Angry. I haven't heard Ema angry in such a long time. "What does it take before you investigate this as what it is?"

The officer gives Ema a condescending smile. "We want to avoid spreading unnecessary fear," he says. "Not every incident has to be a reason to panic. I understand your concerns—"

"You don't understand it at all," Ema says sharply, and the officer looks put off at her tone. He stalks away, and Ema closes her eyes, pulling me close as Kayla leans against me.

I want to tell her that the police are *right* this time—that my dybbuk did this, that we aren't being targeted—but I can't seem to get the words out. The dybbuk has been lying low again since Kayla and I went into the shul last night, and I haven't seen him all morning.

Good, I think. He's wreaked enough havoc for a long time.

I should have finished Kaddish. I should have sent the dybbuk away instead of waking this kind of anger within him. Until now, I've always thought of him as a troublemaker but little else, just a creature trying to get my attention with his mischief. But last night—the shul looked like someone *furious* had done it, someone who wanted to hurt the shul.

I think of the ark in tatters, the siddurim all over the floor, and I suddenly wish that we'd picked them all up last night. The officers aren't going to, and they'll just be *lying* there, dumped across the floor as though they deserved that anger.

I squeeze my eyes shut. It's a Sunday morning, the morning of the Bas Mitzvah Bash, and all I can think about is the siddurim on the floor and the dybbuk staring down at me with dark eyes.

Kayla says, her voice high, "What happens now?"

"The police think the shul will be up and running again by tomorrow. There are volunteers already here to help clean it up, but the police won't let them in." I see them, arguing with the police at the yellow line. A bunch of men I recognize from the shul. The Feigenbaums and the Leibowitzes. And people I don't expect at all—a gaggle of teenagers who aren't dressed in the modest clothes of our community, though some of the boys wear yarmulkes. Two men wearing turbans and a woman in a hijab. A few of the shul's neighbors—a Black couple and a white woman who wave at me when I walk home—stand with the Feigenbaums, fighting loudly with the police.

The police are undeterred. "Not yet," one of them says, loud enough that we can hear it. "We've called in some detectives." He looks irritated with the onlookers. "They'll be able to get a lot more done if the crowd disperses," he says pointedly.

No one moves. I see plenty of my classmates with their families, taking pictures of the shul and speaking worriedly to each other. Behind them is Mrs. Eisenberger, pushing through the crowd as she makes her way toward us. She is dressed for school, rigid and formal, but her shirt is slightly untucked beneath her sweater, her eyes wild as she searches for Kayla. She speaks to an officer, and he waves her through, over the line, so she can run to us.

We all stand up. Mrs. Eisenberger hugs Kayla to her, just like Ema had for me this morning when we saw what was going on. A moment later, she's hugging Ema too, and Ema leans against her shoulder and wraps her arms around Mrs. Eisenberger. I'm the third to be embraced, and it's *nice* feeling like we aren't all on our own, like someone else is with us. "Did you hear anything last night? Do the police have any suspects?" Mrs. Eisenberger asks, rapid-fire. "Are they going to put a weekday guard in front, or—"

"I don't know," Ema says, shaking her head. "The girls were in the shul last night and there was nothing there—"

"We went back," Kayla whispers, and I look down. "Around midnight. The vandals had already been there."

Ema looks at me in astonished betrayal. I barely manage to meet her eyes. "The dybbuk never came back," I try to explain. "So we went to check on him—"

"*Aviva,*" Ema says, and her eyes are wide and pained. "You *can't*—"

"But if it happened last night before midnight," Mrs. Eisenberger says slowly, and she tucks in the loose bit of shirt under her sweater, "why didn't the caretaker report it when he locked up?" She turns to where the shammas is standing with the police, gesturing to the building, and she strides to him.

We follow, bewildered. For once, I'm glad to be walking with Mrs. Eisenberger. She's still scary, but there is something about her that makes me feel safe. "Where were you last night?" she barks out, pointing accusingly at the shammas. "The shul was vandalized before lockup. Why didn't you report it last night?"

The shammas pales. The police look between us, brows furrowing, and I speak up timidly. "We were in the shul around midnight. It wasn't locked. The people had—they'd already did this."

The police chief looks between us, and he says grimly, "Then we have a suspect."

"No!" The shammas looks aghast. "*No,* I didn't—" He glances wildly at us, then back at the shul. "I came at midnight," he admits.

"And as soon as I saw—I *ran*," he says dully. "I locked every door from the outside and ran from the shul. I couldn't—" He closes his eyes. Ema lets out a strangled noise. My stomach hurts, and I don't let myself think about why. "After the last time this happened—" He looks pleadingly at the officers. "I have a family," he murmurs. "I have—people counting on me. I couldn't stay there. I panicked."

"You did the right thing." It's Ema who speaks, her voice quiet but calm. She's white-faced and stricken, but she offers the shammas a weak smile. "You did what you had to do."

"You slowed down this investigation even more," the chief corrects Ema, but he contemplates the shul doors. "So we have a timetable for when this happened, and the doors were locked from the outside of the crime scene until the rabbi called us here this morning. No one broke in. They just . . . walked right in." He considers this, turning to the other officers.

We drift away from them again, back to the mikvah doors. I still feel sick to my stomach, and Kayla is the one to say quietly, "We have to go set up the arcade. The Bas Mitzvah Bash is today."

I blink at her. I almost forgot it in this morning's excitement.

Ema hesitates, and Mrs. Eisenberger says briskly, "I'll bring the girls to the arcade this morning. We'll have to come back to change and get the Jell-O anyway, won't we?" The Jell-O has to be refrigerated right up until the Bash begins, and it's all safe in the laundry room fridge for now. We tried some last night before we went to bed, and it was perfect. "I can give you a ride later."

Ema nods, managing a smile, though it seems feeble to my

eyes. "Thank you," she says, and I know suddenly, with a sinking feeling, that Ema isn't going to make it to the Bash after all.

••

Setting up the clues takes *hours*, and not only because we have to hold out on some of the clues until the arcade empties of visitors. We talk to Kevin, the teenager in charge of the arcade tonight, and he shows us where everything we need will be. He seems just as excited for this as we are. "Just make sure you double-check all the clues you've taped up before your friends come," he warns us. "If you need to reprint any, I'll be in the office."

We weave between the last few teenagers at the arcade, stuffing one clue into the hole of a bowling ball and taping another to the underside of the machine that counts tickets. There are workers setting up a big open space where the arcade restaurant usually is, pushing tables to the side and preparing a big main table for the catered food from a kosher restaurant. The bounce houses have been deflated and removed, cleared for a dance floor.

It's beginning to look more and more like the Bash I always dreamed of, and I'm getting antsy by the time Mrs. Eisenberger says, "I think we'd better head home and get ready for the Bash." She smiles warmly at both of us. "You've got a big night ahead of you. Best to be dressed for it."

She drives me back home, where I can see the yellow tape still up around the shul. The crowd is gone, but police officers still filter in and out. The volunteers are also on the grounds, carrying out destroyed pieces of wood for recycling.

I walk past them, feeling that indescribable shiver pass through me whenever I look at the yellow police lines. The dybbuk did this, wreaked the kind of havoc that can terrify a whole town. I'm so *furious* with him, with everything he's been doing lately, and I glare at the window of the shul where I last saw him and stomp into the mikvah.

"Ema?" No answer. She must be upstairs.

I find her lying under her covers, curled into a ball, her face tearstained and still ashen. "Ema," I whisper, and I climb into the bed beside her, slipping my arms around her and laying my head against her back.

"Is it . . ." Ema croaks. "Is it already time for . . ."

I forget all my plans for tonight, the whole Bash and the scavenger hunt and bringing Ema along. I can't resent Ema for this, not when her pain is palpable, filling the room until all I can think about is the police in front of the shul and the fear—too familiar to be new—that washes over us now. "No," I say shakily. "It's fine. I don't think I'm going to go."

"No," Ema whispers, and she twists around under the blanket to stare at me with red eyes. "You worked so hard on this. I want to see you shine—"

"I'm not feeling great," I choke out, and I try to smile. It feels strained, like I've stretched my mouth but forgotten how to curve it. "I think planning it is way more fun than actually *doing* it. We aren't going to get to be a part of the scavenger hunt anyway. I don't want to go."

"You have to—" Ema begins, but she's so tired. I can see it in the way her eyelids droop, in how she can barely lift her head to look at me. And I know that coming to the Bash is going to be painful for her, and I can't ask it of her.

It's easier to remember I don't really have friends at school anyway—that I've spent two Sundays at the arcade in the past month, and I don't need to spend a night there with a bunch of girls who won't have anything to say to me. It's easy to remember that tomorrow is the big machanayim game and I'm missing that too, and why should I put so much work into the event that is supposed to be my punishment?

It's easy to remember *Ema needs me* and *we're fine* and sitting on the steps of the shul a few weeks ago like there was something compelling me to stay there. I can feel that dark cavern in my heart widening and deepening, threatening to swallow me up, and I gulp in a sob.

I mask it as a cough. "You should sleep, Ema," I whisper, and Ema closes her eyes gratefully, hugging me close, and we drift off.

I dream of the shul, of the shammas entering the shul and seeing the vandals—but this time, I'm there too, and he doesn't run away. Instead there is screaming and fighting, and helpless tears are running down my cheeks, and Mrs. Leibowitz says, "Absolutely *not*."

Yes, I say in my dream. *Yes, this is how it went*—The dybbuk watches me gravely from the top window, and I look to him, beg him to speak.

He speaks in Kayla's voice. "Aviva," he says sharply. "Aviva, wake *up*."

My eyes flutter open, and I realize in horror that I didn't dream Kayla *or* Mrs. Leibowitz. They're both standing in Ema's bedroom, gazing down at us with equal looks of dismay on their faces. "Aviva," Kayla says urgently. "The dybbuk unplugged the fridge."

"*What?*" I stumble out of bed as Ema stirs beside me. "What do you mean the dybbuk unplugged the fridge?"

"It was cold last night, right?" Kayla says, remembering. "We tried the Jell-O, and it was solid and cold. Can Jell-O really go bad?"

Mrs. Eisenberger says from behind her, "I don't think so. It's just an extra precaution. Why don't you two load up the car?"

I shake my head. "I'm not coming with you," I say, and I sneak a look back at Ema. Ema is staring up at the women standing over her, her eyes still bleary and her face still pale. "I'll help put the Jell-O in the car, but I don't want to go to the Bash—"

Kayla stares at me. "Don't be ridiculous," Mrs. Eisenberger says sharply. "Go. Get changed. We're leaving in ten minutes."

Mrs. Leibowitz smiles at me, as grimly determined as Mrs. Eisenberger. Mrs. Eisenberger always dresses like she's about to give a gaggle of eighth graders a stern look, but Mrs. Leibowitz always looks a little funny when she's dressed up in a sheitel and nice clothes, like she's pretending to be something she's not. But today, they are both authoritative and unrelenting. I stare at them, torn, and I suddenly want to cry. I don't *want* to go, not without Ema, not to be the only girl without a parent present. I don't want to force Ema to go either, when she's going to be miserable and the past hangs over us today more than ever—

"Shoshie," Mrs. Eisenberger murmurs, and she takes Ema's hands and crouches in front of her. There's the same gentleness in her voice as when she speaks to Kayla, and Ema lets out a sob.

"I'm sorry," she whispers. "I can't. I wish I—"

"You will," Mrs. Eisenberger says forcefully. "I've left you alone in this apartment for long enough. No more." Ema's hand tightens in Mrs. Eisenberger's, and I watch them, my heart beating rapidly.

Mrs. Leibowitz ushers Kayla and me from the room. "Give her a few minutes," she says, and she turns to Kayla. "Get started on the Jell-O," she says, winking. "No one will ever know the difference."

She leads the way into my room, peering through my closet, and I finally think to say, "What are you doing here?"

"I was cleaning up at the shul when I saw Kayla and her mother trying to get into the mikvah," Mrs. Leibowitz explains. "And I remembered some of the conversations we've had. Aviva," she says, and she pulls a dress from my closet. It's the one I got for Sukkot from a clothing drive, a pretty print dress with multicolored flowers on it. "You aren't the parent here. It's okay to need things sometimes."

"I don't need anything," I say stubbornly, pulling out a plain white shirt to wear beneath the sleeveless dress. "I'm fine. I'm always fine."

Mrs. Leibowitz passes me the dress and goes to the door, her eyes serious. "It's okay to need your mother," she murmurs, and she closes the door behind her as I stare blankly at the dress in my hands.

Chapter 15

EMA IS ALSO DRESSED WHEN I come downstairs. She's wearing one of her nicest Shabbos dresses, a black dress tied with a silver sash she rarely wears anymore, and she's balancing a tray of suspiciously liquidy Jell-O to Mrs. Eisenberger's minivan. "Ema," I whisper, and Ema gives me a tremulous smile. She has wrapped her hair in a tichel with glittery patterns etched across the front, and she looks pretty even without the makeup the other women are wearing.

We pack up the minivan until every tray of Jell-O is secure in the back row, and Kayla and I sit in the middle row as Mrs. Eisenberger drives very slowly toward the arcade. My mood has shifted, lightened with Ema in the seat in front of me, and Kayla is just as enthusiastic. "This is *great*," she says, bouncing. "It almost makes up for missing machanayim tomorrow when we're about to have a night like tonight, but—"

"*Nothing* makes up for missing machanayim tomorrow," we both say together, and we laugh, giddy with excitement. Ema twists around to give me a glowing smile, and I can't believe how *happy* I am, heading to the Bas Mitzvah Bash with my best friend and my mother. I never imagined any of this could happen.

Today is *perfect*, if not for the havoc the dybbuk wreaked at the shul. And the unplugged fridge. I shoot a glare at the Jell-O, a nasty feeling at the pit of my stomach again.

I push it away. I'm not going to let the dybbuk destroy this too.

The arcade is already booming with music when we make our way inside, bringing the Jell-O to the table. Hebrew music is playing from the dance floor, and crowds of girls and their mothers are spinning in circles together. Others are wandering throughout the arcade, taking advantage of the unlimited play.

Shira runs to us when we enter, grabbing Kayla's hand. "Kayla! Come on, let's do *Dance Dance Revolution*—"

Kayla looks apologetic. "I have to set up the Jell-O—it's a long story," she says hastily, and Shira's face begins to fall.

I don't like Shira. I've never liked Shira, not since Kayla and I stopped being friends and she dived in to take my place as though I was never there. She has always been more hostile toward me when other girls were just uncomfortable, and she has only gotten worse lately. But I feel a sudden wave of compassion for her, and it's been a good enough day that I say, "Do you want to help us out?"

Shira brightens, daring a tentative smile at me. Her eyes go wide when she sees Ema, looking very overwhelmed and a hint of glassiness in her eyes, and Shira says, "Yeah, I do!"

Mrs. Eisenberger puts a hand on Ema's back. "The girls have it under control," she says. "Why don't we sit down and get some tea?"

Shira is bursting with enthusiasm, chattering on about the Bash so far. "Everyone's *so* excited for the scavenger hunt," she says.

"We know there's some kind of twist, but Morah Miller won't tell us what—"

"You're going to love it," Kayla promises, and she looks at me, seeking permission, before she confides in Shira, "We found this secret passageway under the mikvah, and it really got us thinking—"

"A secret passageway?" Shira echoes, her eyes round. "That's so *cool*."

I'm still feeling generous. Maybe it's just because I can see Ema sitting at one of the tables when we come in with the Jell-O, sipping tea and chatting with a few other mothers. She is shaking a little bit, awkward and stilted, but Mrs. Eisenberger keeps a hand on hers with that commanding presence. "Maybe you can come by sometime and see it," I suggest, setting down my Jell-O tray on an open table. In the dim lighting, you can't see that it doesn't look quite right.

Shira leans forward, grasping my hand. "Could I really?" She looks suddenly ashamed. "I'm sorry about what I said the other day. You're just... you know," she says, looking around for a moment. Kayla has been distracted by another friend, chatting with her just outside the restaurant, and Shira looks at her and then back at me. "You're a lot cooler than I am," she mutters, looking embarrassed. "And prettier and smarter and I just... I don't want to lose Kayla, you know? It's not like I have any other friends."

I don't know how to respond to that. I didn't know anyone thought of me as *cool* in the first place. But I offer her a smile and I say, "You could have other friends too." It's an invitation I'm not sure I mean, but Shira's eyes glow and she bounces as we head back to the minivan for more Jell-O.

When we're done, I settle in beside Ema at her table. She's talking to Morah Miller, who beams at me when I sit down. "Did you know that your mother was my eighth grade English teacher? One of the best teachers I've ever had."

Ema's cheeks are pink. "It was a long time ago," she says, but she smiles. "And you were one of my favorite students. I used to send you out for a walk at least once a *week*. You could never stop moving."

Morah Miller snorts. I look at them, astonished. "Is that why—is that where you got that from?" I ask Morah Miller, thinking back to the dozens of times I've been sent for a walk this year.

Morah Miller winks at me. "Why don't you go show your mother some of the games here? I think we'll start the scavenger hunt in about an hour."

Ema stands up. She takes a shuddering breath, then a second, and her hands grip the table like it's a lifeboat. The music is loud around us, and I can see Ema's wince at it, the way she has to grit her teeth and then inhale again before she can let go of the table. But then she grins, wiping away her exhaustion, and she says, "What's this I hear about *Dance Dance Revolution*?"

We play four times, and I win the first time and never again. We shoot at zombies at the next game and play the *Let's Make a Deal* game and Ema even puts in a bunch of coins at one of the few machines that aren't unlimited. It's a claw machine, and she has a *gift* for it, snagging a stuffed animal for me on her very first try.

Next is laser tag, and Kayla and her mother team up with us to *crush* a team made up of Esther and Reena and their mothers—when I see Morah Miller motioning to us from the restaurant area. "It's time," I say breathlessly, and I jog across the room with Kayla.

"Okay!" Kayla bellows as girls and mothers begin to filter toward the Jell-O table. She climbs onto a chair. "Listen up! Each color Jell-O is a different team, so make sure you organize before you eat it. You'll find your first clue inside."

I slip away from the crowd, into the back office where Kevin is waiting. "This is the switch you want to flick," he says, showing me what to press. I glance through the office window and see the crush of players moving around Kayla, picking out their Jell-O and separating into groups.

I wait until Kayla gives me the signal that every group has read their clues, and then I say, "Go!"

Kevin hits a button to shut off the music. The room goes abruptly silent. Kevin presses another button, playing a maniacal laugh he'd found on his phone. "*HAHAHAHAHA*," it sounds, and I flip the switch at last.

The room goes dark but for the light of the arcade games glowing dimly. Kevin plays the sound again. "*HAHAHAHAHA*," it repeats. Someone screams, and I lean over the microphone and laugh with it, speaking hastily in a low voice. "*THERE IS A DYB-BUK IN YOUR MIDST*," I say, hearing it broadcast over the room. "*AND SHE'S ALREADY BEGUN TO SABOTAGE YOU.*"

Kayla is still on her chair, and I emerge from the office, stumbling in the dark as she calls out instructions. "Your first clue will come with two flashlights for your team!" she reminds the players. "Be careful who you trust. Every team has a secret dybbuk!"

I make my way to her as the teams spread out, wandering through the arcade as they hunt for clues. Kayla is lit only by the arcade lights, a ghostly figure, and I grab her leg. She shrieks. "It's just me!" I hiss, helping her down and leading her back to Ema's table.

"Oh." Kayla laughs shakily. "This is *amazing*." It really is. The groups are moving in the dark, laughing and shrieking too. "People really do just want to be terrified."

"I want to be terrified," I say wistfully. "I want to get to do this as a *player* next time."

"There are those escape rooms everywhere these days," Mrs. Eisenberger says, sipping her tea. Her phone is upside-down on the table, the flashlight on to illuminate the area a little bit. "Maybe the four of us could pick one out like this and do it together during Pesach vacation."

"Could we?" I say eagerly, looking at Ema. Ema gives me a weak smile. "I mean, sometime, if not Passover," I say hastily. I think I've exhausted Ema enough for a whole year.

Mrs. Eisenberger changes the subject. "I'm surprised Sima Leibowitz didn't come to the Bash," she says. "She told me she'd be here in time for the scavenger hunt." Her brow creases. "Maybe she'll make it for the dancing at the end."

"I hope so," Ema murmurs. "She's been . . . she's a good friend to me." She looks distant for a moment, like she's miles away. "Thank you for bringing me here, Nurit."

"Thank our daughters for doing such a stellar job," Mrs. Eisenberger says. "We couldn't miss *this*." She gestures at the darkened room, the whirr of activity throughout it. There are murmurs and hushed arguments and more than a few yelps as people bang into each other, and then a sudden shout of excitement rising as the first flashlight switches on. It's a ghostly light in the room, bouncing off game screens and thin neon lights.

Ema nods and smiles. "How *did* you two get chosen to plan this event anyway?" she asks. Kayla and I exchange a loaded glance. Ema narrows her eyes. "Do I want to know?"

Mrs. Eisenberger, who works in the school and must know exactly why we were chosen, says, "No. No, you do not." But she gives us another rare smile, the kind that has students jockeying for her approval in eighth grade. "I think Principal Axelrod saw something in you, though. This was a huge project for two sixth graders to tackle on their own. And you've done well."

I blush in the dark, pleased. Kayla beams. Ema says, "I'm glad I'm here to see it." She gives me a tired smile, one so proud that I am breathless with it.

"It reminds me of the pranks we used to play on the girls for Purim," Mrs. Eisenberger says reflectively. "Remember that pop quiz you gave?"

"Remember that time you walked into my class and taught them grammar for fifteen minutes straight before someone had the nerve to ask what you were doing there?" Ema leans forward. "She would pull off *so* many pranks on her students because no one could read her deadpan. They always took her a little too seriously."

Mrs. Eisenberger laughs. It's the first time I've seen her laugh in years, and I watch, astonished, as she and Ema lean in to gossip together about some of what Ema's missed for the past five years.

Kayla and I are quiet, listening avidly to their adventures as flashlights swing around the room and groups dash past us in search of clues. We exchange a secret smile in the dim light, a quiet feeling of *rightness* that seems to settle across the room. This is how things should be, our families and friendship and the Bas Mitzvah Bash we should have been waiting for all along.

The very last clue for all seven groups is located in the office with Kevin, a paper that invites the winning team to turn on the lights and the music again, and we jump up when the music begins and the lights flicker back on. Esther is in the winning group, crowing with her teammates in her high-pitched voice as they head to the dance floor, and I tug Ema's hand. "Dance with me," I say without thinking.

It's too much, and I know it already. The dance floor is already loud, the winning team moving in an exuberant circle as other teams begin to join them, and Ema isn't cut out for that kind of noise and enthusiasm. Still, this might be the only chance we can have for a while.

"It's okay to need your mother," Mrs. Leibowitz said. I wonder where she is and if she'll come soon so we can dance with her too. And Ema takes my hand with some trepidation and walks with me to the dance floor.

We dance together, just the two of us at first, and then Kayla is grasping my hand and her mother has another mother's hand and we're spinning in a spiral of girls and women, round and round until I'm exhilarated and laughing and free. We let hands go to fall into the familiar steps to every Bas Mitzvah dance, our feet moving nimbly without ever quite matching the person's beside us. I don't even know what dance I'm supposed to be doing, only that I'm moving and clapping in time with everyone else, and it feels like, for the first time, that I'm really a part of all of this.

I almost want to cry. I almost want to sing along. Instead, I bask in the glow of Ema's smile, of my classmates as they mouth *so much fun!* and *that was amazing!* to Kayla and me as they dance past. I bask in *joy*, in this circle of Jewish women—of *other* Jewish women, just like me—in a single night, a group united in the same song and dance regardless of our ages and our experiences.

I'm still grinning as we climb into the car with the Eisenbergers much later, Kayla and I curled up together in the middle row and Ema dozing off in the passenger seat. It's been a long, wonderful night, and I can't stop talking. "Did you hear what Hodaya's mother said about the scavenger hunt? She couldn't stop raving about it."

"I heard Hodaya throwing up in the bathroom after that," Kayla says, and she pulls a face. "I *hope* that wasn't our Jell-O."

"Your mother was the one to tell us to use it anyway," I remind Kayla. "It's not *our* fault if the Jell-O was bad."

"We can blame a dybbuk. They'll never know which." Kayla cackles, and I wonder suddenly about my dybbuk back at home. *Is the dybbuk home again? Has he found new ways to destroy the shul?* "Maryam also looked a little green. I hope she's okay for the machanayim game tomorrow."

"We have the morning free," I remind Kayla. "Plenty of time

to sleep off the Jell-O. *Hopefully.*" We giggle again, giddy as Mrs. Eisenberger pulls up in front of our apartment. The yellow tape is still up in front of the shul, and she stops right before it so we can step out easily.

But almost immediately, I see something is wrong. The police officers are still arrayed around the shul, the cars off and the lawn well lit, but it isn't them that we see right away.

No, it's the flashing red lights ahead, the movement around the ambulance that has my heart stopping. I break away from Ema as the Eisenbergers drive off, tearing across the lawn as Ema calls my name. Somehow, I already know.

The dybbuk has done something else. The dybbuk is lashing out, and he's no longer a friendly, familiar presence. He's a villain, and I'm the only one who knows it. "What did he do?" I shout, and I must sound like I've lost my mind, a kid running across the grass in formalwear in the middle of the night. "Who did he—"

I see Mrs. Leibowitz on the stretcher, and my heart stops.

Chapter 16

"THEY THINK IT'S PROBABLY JUST A broken leg," Mrs. Leibowitz says as I stare at her in horror. She looks as though she's in a lot of pain, her forehead all crumpled up and her breathing unsteady. Ema is behind me now, a hand on my shoulder. She's shaking, and I can feel it against my skin. "I was helping move some bookcases when one came down on me out of nowhere. I haven't missed the whole Bas Mitzvah Bash, have I?"

Ema doesn't respond. I turn and I see she's shut down, her eyes glassy and her face white as a ghost. Mrs. Leibowitz reaches for her hand, grips it while Ema trembles, and I can see the tears slipping down her face as she struggles to breathe.

Mrs. Leibowitz says softly, "Shoshie—" and Ema takes a step forward and then stops again, unmoving. Then we're shooed away by the EMTs. They move Mrs. Leibowitz into the ambulance and climb inside. Her husband ducks in behind her, his salt-and-pepper beard and flash of a white button-down shirt the last thing I see before the ambulance takes off, the red lights whirling rapidly as it drives silently through the night.

I'm still frozen under Ema's hand. *One came down on me out of nowhere.* Not out of nowhere, never out of nowhere. The dybbuk pushed a bookcase on Mrs. Leibowitz. And he *knows* her, just like I do. She's a mikvah visitor, one he's created chaos for before, but never like this.

It could have been Mrs. Feigenbaum instead, I realize in horror, who is old and frail and might have been hurt much more by the dybbuk. I've never seen him angry before now, and I don't know what he's capable of.

Was it Kaddish that made him so furious? I think back to the frenzied way the dybbuk swooped at us when we said the words to make him go away. But *no*, he was swooping around like that even earlier, back when Kayla and I were in the mikvah eating marshmallows and chocolate chips.

Maybe it isn't Kaddish that's made him angry. Maybe it was when we went into the passageway, his secret home. Or maybe it was just me, another fixture of the mikvah like Ema and the dybbuk, venturing out into the world. Making *friends*. Doing something other than sitting inside and trying not to be sad.

To the dybbuk, my happiness is unacceptable.

I can feel my own fury beginning to rise to match the dybbuk's. Is that all he wants? Does he want me lonely and alone? Does he lash out at the thought of having to share me with the world? I'm not *his!*

I clench my fists. *Enough*, I decide. *Enough*. I'm going to do what I should have done a long time ago.

Beside me, Ema swallows. "We have to . . ." she begins, and then she falters. We walk across the lawn, closer to the people moving in and out of the shul. Ema's steps are cautious, mine determined, and I squeeze my fingernails into my palm as Ema clears her throat.

One of the volunteers—the woman in the hijab, joined by a few teenagers—blinks up at her, her face kind. "My daughter and I want to help out," Ema whispers, gesturing at me. "If there's anything we can do . . ."

The shul is no longer a mess, but it's not the way it should be either. The wrongness hits me from the moment we step inside, from the moment I look around at the regal building and find it empty. The broken bookcases and pews are gone, the curtains tucked away for the garbage, and the shattered windows have been swept up and covered in plastic for now.

But with them goes the sense of majesty and holiness that has always suffused the shul, the feeling of being a part of something mighty and good. This is a building brought to its knees by a vengeful dybbuk, and tears spring to my eyes as I crane my neck and look around.

The dybbuk, of course, is nowhere to be found, returned to hiding after the way he's hurt so many people. My fists are still squeezed together, my heart pounding with fury, and I walk mechanically through the shul, my eyes narrowing at every flash of movement that might be him.

But it never is. Maybe he's gone back to the mikvah, but I don't think so. He'd revel in this confusion, would lurk in hiding to mock the good people trying to fix what he destroyed. He's still somewhere here, and I suddenly know where.

I walk over to a tall, bearded man with dusty clothes who is clearing out rubble, and I gesture at the stacks of torn, ruined siddurim on a pew. "Can I bring those down to the genizah?" I say.

He glances at me, distracted. "Yeah, sure, that'd be a great help," he says, turning back to the mess in front of him. I pick up loose papers and destroyed siddurim, carrying them carefully to the unobtrusive door at the corner of the women's section of the shul.

I flick on the light switch and walk down the stairs, balancing the papers in my arms, and I hiss, "Dybbuk, come *out* here." The lights are flickering, slowly turning on in the genizah, and I say it louder. "Dybbuk!"

Nothing. But if he's in the passageway, then he won't hear me from the stairs.

I reach the bottom of the stairs. The lights are still going on and off, unsettled, and the tall piles of texts in the genizah look like shadowy mountains from here. I can see a second door in the light, the one that leads to the rest of the basement, and I almost miss the door Kayla and I entered through in the first place.

I set down my pile of papers, and I spot, right near the top, a scrap of paper from a siddur with Kaddish written on it. There are probably a hundred pages like that in every siddur. Still, it feels like a sign.

I clench it in my hand, picking through the piles of Hebrew-inscribed paper until I finally make it to the door to the passageway, half-hidden behind the mounds of paper. Carefully, I seize the door and yank it open, stepping out into the dim passageway. "Dybbuk!" I call out.

No answer but a flicker of movement deep in the passageway. "I know you're there," I say, stepping forward. The light coming in from the genizah means I can see the shape of the passageway here, the bend in it up ahead.

The farther in I walk, the less I can see, and I don't care. "Dybbuk!" I shout. Nothing but the slightest movement up ahead of me. "Get out here, you coward! *DYBBUK!*"

He's moving away from me, and I press my hand against the side of the passageway to find my way, feeling a twinge of fear. I'm all alone down here, and no one will know where I've gone. If the dybbuk really has lost control, then he's going to be unpredictable, and I'm on my own against him.

I can handle him. I've always been the one to handle him. I can't read the paper in my trembling hand, but I know the Kaddish from memory, from the dozen times it's read every Shabbos in the shul. *"Yisgadal v'Yiskadash Shemei Raba,"* I begin, and I imagine voices, like a ghostly *"Amen"* as I speak. *"B'alma di vra kirutei."*

Something is happening. I say the next words as I creep forward, closing in on the dybbuk as I sense him nearing me. I'm shivering, and I know I'm terrified and furious at once, determined to stop the dybbuk, and I say the response we always say together in shul aloud. *"Amen! Yehei shmei raba mevorach l'alam ul'almai alma—"*

Something hard hits me. I react without thinking, hurtling forward, and for the first time in nearly six years, the dybbuk is solid in front of me.

But this time, he isn't pulling me from the mikvah pool to safety.

He swings a fist at me and hits me in the gut, and I flail, my fists crashing into his and my heart pounding. The dybbuk is trying to *hurt* me, hurt me like he hurt Mrs. Leibowitz and our entire community, and I choke at the force of his blow.

He can't stop me. He has to be stopped, and I gather all my strength and leap at him, scrabbling at eyes that aren't real and yanking at long hair that can't possibly be real either. He lets out a howl of pain, the very first noise I've ever heard from him.

It reminds me of what I'm doing, of how I can get rid of him for good. "*Yisbarach v'yishtabach v'yispa'ar v'yisromam v'yisnasei,*" I grit out desperately, beating at his chest and his arms. I knee him in the gut and punch him again, with all the force I use when I hurl a machanayim ball, and he lets out a stunned, furious sound, and then beats at me with his fists.

I panic, bruised and stunned, and I detach from him and run. I don't know where I'm going, whether it's back to the genizah or toward the mikvah. The winding, pitch-black passageways all look the same to me, and I bang against walls and turn, stumbling away as he gives chase. "*V'yishadar v'yisaleh v'yishalal shmei d'kudsha, brich hu,*" I gasp in a whisper, running onward. The dybbuk pursues me, silent again, and I can feel his malice filling the passageway.

He's hurt me. He might even *kill* me, I realize in horror, and I echo myself, terrified, "*Brich hu!*" He can't kill me. Someone will realize that I'm gone soon, and they know I went to the genizah. Someone will find us before it's too late. And then they'll understand everything, exactly who did this to us—

I crash into a wall—a stone wall, reaching high above me, and I understand suddenly that I've gone in the wrong direction. In front of me is the wall of the draining pool. I ran to the mikvah side, and the door in the mikvah will never open when the mikvah is full. The water pressure keeps it sealed, impossible to open.

I'm trapped, cornered at the wall of my house. I scrabble for the door of the mikvah and find it flat, no door handle or anything but an unobtrusive rectangle high in the wall I can feel against my hands. I recite as much of the Kaddish as I can, this time determined to finish before the dybbuk gets to me.

He's getting closer. "Little *brat*," he spits out, and I can hear his footfalls coming closer and closer, nearly at the end of the passageway. His voice is lower than I thought it would be, angrier and more menacing, and I can only whisper the desperate words in Aramaic, a language used by my people only in learning and davening. "*Y'hei shlama raba min shimaya v'chayim aleinu v'al kol yisrael, v'imru amen*," I say, and I'm sobbing, terrified of what the dybbuk might do to me and terrified of what might happen if the dybbuk disappears now.

I can hear the dybbuk's ragged breath, his furious steps, and he's so close—it'll only be a few more steps before he's on me. "They're never going to find your body," he snarls, and I can only think of one reckless, impossible option.

"*Oseh shalom bimromav*," I say, and I'm terrified as I twist around, my back to the dybbuk so I'm defenseless. "*Hu ya'aseh shalom aleinu v'al kol yisrael*," I breathe, and I press my hands flat against the door on the mikvah wall.

"Stop it," the dybbuk snaps. "Stop chanting, little girl."

With all my might, I push, push, against hundreds of gallons of water forcing the door to stay in place underwater, against an impossible task, and I gasp out, "*V'imru amen.*"

Amen, I think, or maybe I hear myself whisper it in an echo, and as I push, I can feel my strength growing. It feels almost as though I'm not on my own, as though someone is pushing the door with me, pressing against the door with more power than I'll ever have.

"*SHUT UP!*" the dybbuk roars, and Kaddish didn't work. He's still here. He's upon me, his hands grabbing my arms.

And something incredible happens. The door opens, first a tiny fraction of an inch, and then halfway, *all the way*, and water pours from it in an enormous rush, passing over my head and crashing into the dybbuk in an enormous current. It blows him right off of me, back into the passageway as the water empties out of the mikvah in waves, faster than the drain has ever worked.

I don't look back. I scramble out of the mikvah as the water pours from it and the dybbuk shouts. I slam the door closed and I scream at the top of my lungs, scream and scream a piercing shout that is too high and shrill for me to recognize. I race up the empty steps of the mikvah in my soaked dress and matted hair, hurtling from the pool and toward the door to outside, still screaming as loudly as I can as police officers and volunteers alike all rush toward me, the lawn outside the mikvah brighter than it's ever been at night.

"It was the dybbuk!" I cry out as they gather around me. "It was the dybbuk, it was the dybbuk, he tried to *kill* me!"

"No," someone says, and I see Ema through tearstained eyes, crouched in front of me as a dozen people stand around us, demanding answers. "No, Aviva—"

"I saw him!" My voice is garbled as I shout, still high and panicked. "I have to stop him! He was under the mikvah—the dybbuk—"

"There is no dybbuk! There was never a dybbuk!" Ema shouts, and I fall silent at last, my eyes wide.

And Ema begins to weep.

Chapter 17

THERE IS NO DYBBUK. NOT IN the passageway anyway. The police go in and find a shell-shocked man with angry eyes who is cuffed and carried away. "He must have been trapped inside when the caretaker locked up the synagogue," the chief says to us as he's led off. "He found a place and hid there, waiting for the synagogue to empty out so he could escape. I don't think he expected anyone to be wandering in a passage underground."

He shakes his head. "He's already admitted to vandalizing the synagogue with a few friends, but he's adamant that he had nothing to do with the symbol on the sidewalk. I don't think we'll ever find out who drew it."

"Edgy teenagers," Ema says, and if it's a little bitter, the police chief doesn't acknowledge it. I stand next to Ema, my hand tight in hers, and we don't move as the officers depart.

"They'll keep an eye out for a few weeks," says a voice beside us. Mrs. Feigenbaum has hobbled over, leaning on her cane as she joins us. "Make sure there are no copycats inspired by him. Then they'll find his friends and arrest them and declare anti-Semitism a relic of the Middle Ages again." She offers us a humorless smile, her eyes sweeping over me. "Ach, zeeskeit, you're soaking wet!"

"Oh!" Ema startles as though she's only just realized. "Let's go inside, Aviva, so you can get in pajamas."

I still can't speak, can't demand the answers I crave. *There is no dybbuk! There was never a dybbuk!*

When I walk inside, the dybbuk is sitting alone in the waiting room of the mikvah, his eyes sightless. He doesn't acknowledge me, and I say silently, *Ema is wrong. Here you are.*

I change into pajamas. When I come back downstairs, Mrs. Feigenbaum and Ema are having tea in the waiting room, the dybbuk watchful beside Ema. I sit opposite her and say blankly, "The dybbuk is sitting next to you."

"No," Ema says, and she's red-eyed, ready to cry again. "No, it isn't. It isn't real, Aviva. And I shouldn't have let this go on for so long—to think you went into that passageway to *find* it—you could have been—" She stops, breathing in a shuddering breath, and Mrs. Feigenbaum gets up and hobbles over to the laundry room to make me some tea too.

"Aviva," Ema says, and she trembles, tucking her feet beneath her and cradling her tea. "Do you remember what happened to Abba?"

"An accident," I say mechanically. I don't talk about what happened to Abba. None of us do because talking about it is almost as bad as experiencing the aftermath again, the months of quiet loneliness after and the horror of that night. I don't like thinking about it either. A cage falls shut around my mind when I try to, as though to force out every intrusive thought. "I was little."

"You were six." Ema squeezes her eyes shut. "Much too young to—" She stops, takes a deep breath. "You were there, Aviva."

I stare at her. "There where?" I wasn't there until *after,* when the ambulance came and the police arrived and the street was blocked off. I remember that part in bits and flashes, horrible moments I never want to fall into again.

Ema opens her eyes, and there is so much sorrow in them that I can't breathe. "Abba used to bring you to the shul with him sometimes, especially on Friday nights when you'd be up late for the Shabbos meal. Do you remember that?"

I remember running around the shul on Friday nights after the meal, when a few men would come to study together in one of the side rooms. I'd stand in front of the podium and pretend to be giving a speech, or I'd perch on a pew and hold on to a lectern and sway like I saw the men do. The shul felt as much a part of my Friday nights as Abba and Ema, and I was joyful in my visits.

I nod warily. "I guess."

"On this Friday night, Abba went to lock up the shul after the study session." Ema looks haunted. "You were with him. I don't know exactly what happened. They have the testimony, but—"

"Testimony," I repeat. I don't remember any of this, and I can feel an odd feeling bubbling up within me, like nausea but worse. It's coming from that cavern in my heart, the one I keep closed up and sealed away. "I don't remember," I say, and the dybbuk tilts his head and watches me solemnly.

But I do. It bubbles up with the nausea, like a dozen tiny knives all digging into me at once. It bubbles up like sitting on the steps of the shul when I was too young to understand, huddled in place and terrified as Abba shouted at—

Kids, they were kids just a few years older than I am now, I think, but they seemed like giants back then. They taunted him, were throwing rocks at the shul, and—

I shake, and I focus on the dybbuk in front of me. I feel sick, and even Mrs. Feigenbaum returning and pressing tea into my hands isn't enough to soothe me. "I don't remember," I choke out again.

Ema watches me in silence, rocking in place as though she doesn't want to be here either. She's crying, the tears slipping down her cheeks, and she says hopelessly, "The shul has always been a target. We have security for Shabbos now, but back then, we hadn't even had that. No one had thought that anyone would really—"

I remember the kids now, remember four or five faces shadowed in the dim light, one with close-cropped hair and another with the shadow of scruff on his face. I remember the way they walked, like someone who had a little too much to drink on Purim, the jerky movements and the shrieking laughter as Abba tried to stop them. I remember a tall one shouting—*get out of our town*—and the scruffy one yelling a word I'd never heard before—*dirty kike*—and all of them calling *Jew Jew Jew* between insults and taunts until it felt like a curse word. I remember staring at them, frozen and terrified, as Abba put himself between them and the shul, between them and me.

It's all a blur from then on. "I don't remember," I whisper, and I *don't*, not which one threw the first punch or how Abba was jumped by them, how they threw his yarmulke and he fought them, how the fight moved to the street and how a car came racing down the street and Abba was all in black in his Shabbos suit, tangled in a fight with a bunch of teenagers too distracted to see the car coming. I don't remember how it happened, only that I was huddled on the stairs just a few dozen feet away from my spot right now, frozen and terrified and all alone.

The driver must have called the police. I remember them coming and trying to urge me into an ambulance, and I remember screaming *It's Shabbos! It's Shabbos! I won't go!* and kicking and screaming when they tried to drive me away. I remember Ema arriving, clutching on to me as she screamed, and then I remember falling very, very silent.

"I remember," I say, and my voice sounds distant, like I'm hearing it through a tunnel. I'm shaking, tears streaming down my face, and Ema drops to the floor in front of me, pleading.

"I wasn't a good mother to you when you needed me," she says, and she quivers, her hands on my knees. "I was . . . I was sad for a very long time. I didn't know how to help you. I didn't know how to help myself either. And you wouldn't—" She inhales a shaky breath. "You wouldn't move. You wouldn't speak. For months, I tried getting you the help you needed, but we were both a mess. I couldn't bring you to doctors after a few weeks, not when it seemed to make you even worse. I couldn't push you because you would shut down even more. It took all I had just to get you to eat."

I put my hands on Ema's. I don't know what else to do. The memories are rumbling through me like a creature finally set free, like images from another lifetime. Abba on that night, lifting me onto his shoulders on the way to the shul, the air rushing against my skin as he moved and the vibration of his deep baritone as he laughed at something I said. The stale air of a psychologist's office, sitting at a table opposite a woman with a pointy face as she pushed puzzle pieces toward me and chatted, her voice too loud and too strident. Ema's arms wrapped around me every night, warm and unsteady, and the blur of pink walls and white furniture that had never been clear again in my mind after that. And the ambulance, the flashing lights at the shul like they'd been earlier tonight, and Abba lying still on a stretcher with his eyes blank and a hand hanging down, swinging as the stretcher moved. I thought then that it was him reaching out for me, that I could just move forward and see him smile at me, and then an EMT tucked Abba's hand back on to his chest and it remained there, limp.

I've never wanted to remember that moment, I know that. I don't remember most of being six years old, just before, and then the mikvah.

Ema has remembered it for the both of us, and I've been terrified of ever becoming like her. "We've never even been to his grave," she sobs. "I can barely—it's like we've been frozen in time, still in the shul five years ago, and I've never been able to leave. And I haven't been a good mother to you—god, I've *wanted* to, but it's like I've forgotten how—"

"*Mamaleh,*" Mrs. Feigenbaum murmurs. I can't say anything, not with Ema knelt on the floor in front of me. I remember Mrs. Leibowitz saying, a few hours and a lifetime ago, *It's okay to need your mother,* and how it felt almost illicit to acknowledge. I want to reassure Ema that she's been everything I needed and has always been a good mother to me, but the words won't emerge. I'm frozen, and I still want to throw up when I think about that night.

Ema shakes her head vigorously. "You didn't *speak*," she bursts out again. "Not for months! Then we moved over the mikvah and just a few days later, you came upstairs and said, 'There's a dybbuk in the mikvah.' It was like you were finally okay. I thought it was a game for you, like an imaginary friend or a fantasy that would distract you from what had happened. At first, you would only speak about the dybbuk. And then one day, you went outside to see if it would follow you there and then to school to test its limits. The dybbuk was the only thing that helped you."

I shake my head, and the dybbuk raises his eyebrows at me, waiting for me to defend his existence. "But there *is* a dybbuk," I say fiercely. "I can see him right now. You've seen what he does—"

"I've seen you spread soap on the bathroom floor," Ema whispers. "I've seen you tear up checks we've received. I've seen you flood the laundry room. There is no dybbuk, Aviva."

"No," I say, and I struggle to remember a single time that I couldn't have—that it *must* have been the dybbuk. In the chair opposite me, the dybbuk flickers, then looks astonished, as though I willed him away. "There was—when I found that passageway, he turned the water back on in the mikvah—"

Or did he? I noticed the handle to turn it on just before Kayla and I went into the passageway. Did I—

I remember padding upstairs with Kayla after we saw the shul trashed, terrified and unnerved, and I said, *be right back,* and then I—

I—

Did I unplug the fridge? I tremble, staring in horror at the dybbuk sitting opposite me, and Ema says beseechingly, "I spoke to professionals, and they told me to let it be. That this was how you were going to process your trauma, and you would age out of it once you were older. I should have—I should have gone back for more advice years ago, but I . . . but then you described the dybbuk to me and I—"

She stands up abruptly, hurrying up the stairs, and I stare at the dybbuk and then Mrs. Feigenbaum. "He's real. I can *see him*." But he's flickering again, coming and going as my certainty wavers, and I choke back another sob.

Ema comes back downstairs, and I see what she's holding. It's a photo album, one I haven't touched since we first moved here. "Your grandparents put this together for you. Do you remember? It's a book of Abba." She blinks back tears and sits beside me, letting me turn the pages.

The first few pages are of Abba and me and Ema, all of us posing together with bright smiles. There are a couple from a department store photoshoot where I look three or four, and Ema glows in them, laughing with Abba. Abba's eyes are bright and he has a neat beard that can't hide the flash of white teeth and the way his chin tips back in a laugh. Others are from the local park near the water, the three of us on a brick-red picnic blanket that is sharp against the green of the grass. I am perched on Abba's lap, tugging at his beard as he grins down at me, and Ema is resting her head against Abba's shoulder.

Then there are some of Abba and Ema at their wedding, most of them posed, but there is one that stands out to me. It's late in the wedding and they're outside in the dark, and it must have been raining because I can see little droplets in the background. Ema and Abba are holding hands and smiling at each other, without a clue of what will happen in nine years. There's a single picture of me as a newborn on that page, snuggled in Abba's arms. He's just beginning to grow the beard I saw in the later pictures, and he looks at me with so much love shining in his eyes that I swallow and stare at it for a long time before I turn the page.

The next page has older pictures, faded and with that odd gloss of pre-digital photos. They're of Abba as a teenager, and there is something very familiar about him, something I don't place until I turn another page and see my dybbuk staring at me from the pages. Abba at eleven. My dybbuk, the same olive skin and pointed nose and mischievous eyes, the same lanky frame the dybbuk and I share.

I look up, and he's smiling sadly at me, and I can't believe it. I can't believe my dybbuk is just my imagination working overtime. The dybbuk has been there for all this time, long after I would have outgrown an imaginary friend. "No," I whisper, and I remember pushing at the mikvah door, the feeling like extra hands on it as I tried to escape from the vandal. "No, it can't be—"

The dybbuk fades away in front of me, just an empty chair as I stare in horror, and I clutch on to the photo album. "Dybbuk," I say faintly.

He doesn't reappear.

"I did . . . I did all the things he'd done?" I wonder, disbelievingly, desolate. What's wrong with me? How could I have done *everything*—and never known it? I think back to ripped-up checks and ruined towels, to all the things I destroyed to keep up a fantasy. "I was the one wrecking the mikvah?"

"Only a little," Ema says fondly, and there's a tremor to her voice even now. "Never anything that couldn't be fixed. And you always cleaned up your messes."

I twist around, looking wide-eyed at Mrs. Feigenbaum with renewed guilt. "But I always blamed the dybbuk! And you all—everyone who came to the mikvah and believed that the dybbuk was real—"

"Zeeskeit," Mrs. Feigenbaum says, and she smiles at me with eyes that have seen more evil and more kindness in this world than anyone else I've ever known. "We always knew."

Chapter 18

IN THE MORNING, EMA AND I sit at the breakfast table in silence. The windows in our rooms are cracked open, and there is the sound of the rustle of leaves drifting in, a breeze tugging lazily at my hair. I can hear school busses driving past and the voices of other kids calling to each other, the whole world moving while Ema and I scrape our spoons into our cereal bowls and wash them off without a word when we're done. We aren't angry or anything— just processing, I guess. A lot has happened in the past day. If we weren't given the morning off after the Bas Mitzvah Bash, I probably would have taken it off anyway.

Outside, I can hear the lilting sounds of davening from the shul, louder than usual through the broken windows. The police tape is still up and an officer is parked outside of the shul, but from the lawn, there's no other visible sign of what happened yesterday. People slow as they walk past the shul, but they continue on, nothing more to see.

Life goes on, no matter what might have happened yesterday. But life hasn't *gone on* for me in years.

I go downstairs after breakfast and walk through the rooms of the mikvah, my eyes dance around in an instinctive search for the dybbuk. I don't know if I expect to see him or not, and I feel an odd flicker of apprehension when there's movement behind me. But it's only a reflection of the clouds parting and the sun outside, shining against the curtains, and I am relieved. The mikvah is silent, untouched, nothing out of place or meddled with. I sink down into one of the chairs in the waiting room, and I wait.

I don't know what I'm waiting for, but it comes anyway. Ema walks down the steps from the mikvah, and I stare. She's wearing a sheitel, a wig she's barely touched in five years, and the hair falls free in waves around her pretty face. She looks at me, and she says, "I thought we might go to visit your father's grave today."

We haven't been to Abba's grave since the month after, during the unveiling. When I think back to the unveiling now, I remember standing stiffly, surrounded by family. I wore a scratchy dress my cousin had outgrown and the cold sensation of Ema's hand in mine. It smelled like wet grass and my aunt's perfume, and my cousins and aunts and uncles hovered around me, closing me in with Ema and the gravestone. Now, I can't remember speaking to any of them at all. I can barely even remember how the cemetery looked. It's all fuzzy, like I was seeing it from afar.

We have to take a bus across New Beacon to the cemetery, and I bring my backpack with me, just in case I have to go straight to school afterward. Ema is quiet on the bus beside me, her hands pressed together and her fingers linked to stop the shaking. Her eyes are still glassy. I don't know if anything has changed for her, not like it did for me last night, but her face is a little less pale in the sunlight, her lips set in a way that makes her look a little more determined. She manages a smile for me, and I put my hand on her knee and watch the streets pass by. Beacon is smaller and older than New Beacon's wide sidewalks and rows of stores, the houses here as big as the shul and the streets green and well-kept.

I wonder how Abba's grave looks now. When I was little, it was so tall I was barely able to reach up to place a rock on top of it. Now, I'm a lot taller, and I can't imagine any situation where Abba doesn't tower over me.

We get off the bus at the stop closest to the cemetery, and I use Ema's phone to navigate the last block to what looks almost like a park until I catch sight of the headstones. There are so many, and I don't know where we'll find Abba. We step into the cemetery, a woman and a girl arriving in the middle of the day, and I think it must be obvious why we're here. Grief hangs around this place like a shroud, and Ema puts a hand on my arm and I exhale.

There is a woman near the front entrance in a blouse and a crisp pair of slacks, and she smiles at us. "Do you need help finding someone?" she asks.

Ema says, "I know the way." I grip her hand as we walk through a winding path, through low grass and past headstones with a familiar Jewish star on them. Each time, I hesitate, trying to read the names, but Ema doesn't stop moving. The air is clean here, a salty tang to it from a nearby body of water, and the path is rough enough I can feel the rockiness against the soles of my shoes.

"Here." Ema lets my hand go and starts ahead of me, leading the way to a row of neat headstones. She looks like someone else from behind, with her sheitel flowing past her shoulders and the neat shirt and skirt she's put on. I hardly recognize her, and this whole place feels as alien to me as Ema's back looks in the sunlight.

The grave is much smaller than I remember, a modest little headstone with Abba's name written on it.

פ׳נ

HERE IS BURIED

אלעזר שמשון בן חיים הי״ד

נפטר ראש חדש שבט תשע״ג

ELAZAR SHIMSHON JACOBS

1981–2013

BELOVED HUSBAND AND FATHER

SHAMMAS TO THE BEACON COMMUNITY

ת.נ.צ.ב.ה.

The one thing that surprises me is the number of rocks resting on top of the headstone. That's one Jewish custom I don't really understand, and I swallow as I see how many rocks lie on top of Abba's. We've never been back, but others have come and paid their respects, so many that there's no space for us to put down rocks of our own.

I go searching for a rock while Ema stands in front of the grave, swaying in silence with her eyes closed. Down along the path a dozen or so yards from the tombstone, I find a little gray stone, perfectly smooth and a little flat.

That's when I start crying. I don't know why, what it is about the perfect little gray stone that makes the cavern in my heart finally crack open. I'm not panicking like I did in the shul, and I can breathe, can feel my chest heave in sobs, tears running salty into my mouth as I crouch on the ground and cry and cry and cry.

I thought the cavern might swallow everything if I left it open, but the walls of it grow around me until they shatter instead, sending little dark fault lines through me. I kneel down, my thumb on the stone, and I sob for a thousand Shabboses without Abba, for our old house and Abba's smile and the way there was space for the two of us on the big chair that was his.

I cry for Abba, who was the best storyteller I knew, who made Ema smile without the slightest hint of sadness. I cry for years of being alone in a tiny apartment, which felt sometimes like disappearing, for the dented brown cardboard of the packages at our door that replaced *people*, for years of Ema being too afraid to let me wander free. I cry and I cry until I run out of reasons to cry, and then I cry because I've wanted to cry for *so long* and been so terrified of what might happen if I did.

Yet nothing happens, except the stone is wet and I feel drained. The sky is still blue above me. Abba is still gone. But I close my fingers around my stone and stand up, and I press the hand with the stone to my heart as I follow the path back to the grave.

I stop as I near it. Ema is still swaying quietly, her lips forming words I can't make out, but it isn't her who's caught my attention. It's a ghostly figure I know, a boy who was all in my head.

My dybbuk is sitting on top of Abba's burial plot, leaning against the headstone, and I hesitate, unsure what I should do. He wiggles his eyebrows at me, gesturing for me to approach, and I want to say, *You're not real—go away!*

But I don't. The dybbuk watches me, and I see there's a space in the center of the headstone that is empty, a clear circle in the midst of all the rocks that weren't there before.

Maybe Ema cleared it for me. Maybe I did it myself without realizing, like I have so many times before. Maybe it was there all along and I didn't see it. Still, it's hard to stand there and pretend that I'm not seeing a boy with Abba's face as he watches me expectantly, waiting for me to set the stone down.

I place my stone in the center of the headstone, and then I press my hand to its side. "Thank you, Abba," I whisper, and then I say a few more things too.

When I turn around, Ema is sitting on a moss-spotted stone bench opposite the grave, and I walk to join her. The dybbuk still lingers on Abba's plot, watching us, but I force my eyes away from him. "Thank you for bringing me here," I say instead.

Ema doesn't respond at first. When she talks, her words are careful. "I think I've been stuck for a long time. And it's time to . . ." She takes a shuddering breath. "Abba would want me to let go of the past," she says. "I know that."

"Not let go," I say, watching the dybbuk again.

"Not entirely, but . . ." Ema swallows. "This morning, I called someone who can help us," she says. "Someone who we can both talk to, if you'd like. Together or apart. I want to go outside more. I want to stop feeling as though—as though every day is a struggle." Ema's never spoken this honestly to me before, and I feel new tears spring to my eyes, a relief from a tension that was so ingrained in my life with Ema that I didn't notice it until it left. "And I'm going to do what I can to work through this. Because it's what you deserve."

"It's what you deserve too," I whisper, and Ema offers me a tearstained smile. I wrap my arm around her waist, and she pulls me close, her arm around my shoulder. "I love you," I murmur.

"I love you," she says fervently, and we stare together at Abba's headstone. I watch as the dybbuk smiles at me. For the first time, I recognize it as Abba's smile, mischievous but warm, and I smile back tremulously. The dybbuk closes his eyes, lifting a hand in a wave farewell, and a wind whips suddenly through the cemetery.

When it passes, the dybbuk is gone, and Ema is smiling again. It's still glassy and fragile, but there is determination behind it, a focus there that wasn't there before. "Let's go home," she says, and she leads the way down the path that winds from the cemetery.

♦♦

We get home with an hour to spare before I have to get to school. Ema makes lunch upstairs while I sit in the mikvah waiting room, kicking a machanayim ball absently against the wall. It bounces back to me and I kick it again. The mikvah is oddly still without the dybbuk flying through it, oddly quiet.

Ema comes downstairs with a plate for each of us, setting them down on the coffee table where we usually only eat on Shabbos. She glances at the machanayim ball. "Next year," she says, sitting down beside me.

"Next year," I repeat, kicking the ball into the laundry room. Machanayim doesn't seem nearly as important after last night, but

I still feel a pang when the ball bounces off the dryer and disappears into the room.

There's a knock at the door as we're finishing our food, and Ema smooths down her skirt, stands up before I can, and opens the door.

Principal Axelrod is standing in the doorway, her eyes light and her smile warm as her familiar perfume wafts through the room. "Shoshie, I am *in awe* of what Aviva and Kayla accomplished last night," she says without preamble. I blush.

Ema smiles. "They're very talented girls," she says. "I'm so proud of them."

"So am I," Principal Axelrod agrees. She beams at me. "You know, Aviva, you have all this *energy* inside of you, and it isn't always . . . *ideal* for a classroom," she finishes delicately. "But part of our Bas Mitzvah is beginning to recognize our gifts and finding the best way to use them."

She turns to Ema. "I was happy to hear that you were at the event last night," she says softly, and Ema is the one to blush now. "I worried when you stopped returning my calls."

Ema meets her eyes. "I didn't know what I could say," she admits. "I wasn't ready to . . . I didn't think I'd ever be ready to come back." She says it in a low voice.

Principal Axelrod nods slowly. "And do you still think that?" she probes, and I understand why Ema might have stopped taking Principal Axelrod's calls. Principal Axelrod has a quality to her, an unspoken demand for every person around her to be *better*, to be the best version of themselves.

Ema takes a breath. "I'd like to," she says. "Be ready to come back, I mean." A shadow crosses her face, and I can see the conflict in her expression, the visible effort to give Principal Axelrod the response she's looking for. Finally, she whispers, "I don't think I am just yet."

"There will always be a place for you in Beacon TDS," Principal Axelrod murmurs. "Just as there has always been a place for Aviva." A thoughtful look crosses her face. "As it turns out, there might be a second one."

I blink. "What does that mean?"

"It's odd," Principal Axelrod says, a twinkle in her eye. "But a number of sixth graders seem to have come down with a light case of food poisoning." I shift guiltily, remembering the Jell-O Mrs. Eisenberger told us to use anyway. "And the four girls chosen as machanayim alternates are *insisting* Kayla Eisenberger and Aviva Jacobs replace them."

I tense, my breath escaping my body. "But you said—"

"I think exceptions can be made after the work you put into the Bas Mitzvah Bash, don't you?" Principal Axelrod says serenely. I gape at her. "Well, I'd better be going," she says, glancing at her watch. "I hope I'll see you both soon." With another smile, she saunters down the path from the mikvah.

Chapter 19

THE SCHOOL IS BURSTING WITH PALPABLE excitement when I walk inside at lunch. I can see half of the middle school already in the gym, crowding the bleachers as they eat their lunches and await the students from HARE, our rival team. The sixth graders are slowly filtering into school, prepared to learn very little today.

Ahuva Rennert, the eighth grade machanayim captain, is tossing a ball back and forth with a few other players, each of them hurling it at another with extra force. Ahuva is the shortest of the bunch, unexpectedly stocky for a star machanayim player, but I know she's good. I've seen the power she can put behind the ball. In the bleachers, students are shouting names and an impromptu school cheer. Principal Axelrod walks along the bleachers with the other teachers, and I even catch sight of Mrs. Leibowitz. She has a boot on one foot, and she's leaning on a wheeled contraption that supports the foot so she can stand. She waves at me, her eyes brightening, and I grin and wave back.

I find Kayla sitting beside a green-looking Shira in the bleachers. She has her backpack on the spot beside her, and she moves it over and gestures wildly for me to join them. "Principal Axelrod said—" she begins breathlessly.

"I know!" We exchange a single ecstatic glance.

"And one of the seventh graders isn't here today. They're calling her house now to find out if she's going to come, but if not—" Kayla rocks in her seat. "Which one of us goes in?"

And suddenly, the machanayim game I was so outraged to be excluded from doesn't seem like nearly as big a deal as anything I've been through lately. I caught a *criminal* last night. My dybbuk isn't real, and it's okay. We put together most of an event on our own yesterday. I'm good at machanayim, but it isn't the only thing I'm good at, and I nod to Kayla. "You should," I say. "We were right. We'll play together next year and finally beat HARE."

Kayla looks reluctant. Shira nudges her. "Come on," she says. "You're both great. Much better than anyone else in the grade. Just go win this." She looks a little sick. "I have to—" Without another word, she scrambles from the bleachers, racing toward the bathroom.

"The dybbuk really poisoned everyone, huh?" Kayla says, nudging me. "I can't believe a little bit of Jell-O did this."

And I remember, with a sinking feeling, that there is something Kayla doesn't know. "The dybbuk isn't real," I say. "I just—I just found out last night. Ema says I kind of conjured him out of nowhere to deal with . . . with Abba."

I brace myself. The whole renewal of our friendship has been built around the dybbuk, around figuring him out and trying to stop him. Without the dybbuk first turning on the shower in the bathroom, we might never have gotten along for long enough to put together the scavenger hunt, let alone to repair our friendship.

Kayla stares at me. "Then who—"

"It was all me. I just . . . I don't think I really knew it. I've been in a weird haze since Abba," I admit. "I didn't want to think about anything I saw back then, and I guess I just . . . stopped thinking about a lot of things. I never meant to—to unplug the fridge or throw your homework in the mikvah or—"

"It's fine," Kayla says without hesitation, and her eyes are bright. "I know you didn't. And the dybbuk still brought us together, didn't it?" She shrugs off the revelation, and her hand lands in mine, squeezing it firmly.

I blink a bunch of times. There's just some dust in my eyes or something that's making them tear up.

A seventh grade player comes running into the gym, hurrying to Ahuva, and I see her nod grimly and scan the bleachers for us. "Go," I say to Kayla. "Win the game. Tell your father all about it when you get home." She looks at me, her lips parted but no words emerging. Finally, her mouth snaps shut, and a determined look settles on her face. She squeezes my hand again and runs out on to the machanayim court.

I watch her go, and I smile.

GLOSSARY

The terms below are common to all four branches of Judaism: Orthodox, Conservative, Reconstructionist, and Reform. However, often pronunciations are different depending on the branch and the community. For instance in some, the final letter (tav or sav) of some words will be pronounced with an *s* sound, in other communities the sound would be *t*. Examples are Bas vs Bat mitzvah, Shabbos vs. Shabbat. In the manuscript and in the glossary below we reflect the pronunciations of the Orthodox community in which Aviva lives.

Abba — Hebrew word for father.

Bas/Bat Mitzvah — a coming of age for Jewish girls at twelve, at which point they gain some spiritual responsibility.

Cossacks — an Eastern European militia that often led pogroms against Jews during the 1600s-1900s.

daven/davening — pray/prayers.

dybbuk — in Jewish folklore, a ghost of a deceased person who returns to complete a certain task.

Ema — Hebrew word for mother.

genizah — a storage place for old holy books, before they're buried in the cemetery.

Gilgul (plural Gilgulim) – in Jewish folklore, a reincarnated soul.

Golem – in Jewish folklore, a Frankenstein's monster created to protect a Jewish community.

hatzlacha – good luck.

Kaddish – a prayer for the deceased said various times during prayers.

kiddush – both a prayer said before drinking grape juice or wine and a buffet served after prayers on Sabbath, in which the above prayer is said.

machanayim – a ball game played in some Jewish schools and camps.

mamaleh – a Yiddish word for a little girl (little mama).

mikvah – a pool used for religious immersing.

Morah – an honorific meaning teacher.

ner tamid – "eternal candle," a special light in the synagogue.

Shabbos – Saturday, a day of rest for observant Jews.

shammas – caretaker of a synagogue.

sheidim – Demons in Jewish mythology.

sheitel – a wig worn by some married (and once-married) Jewish women.

sheket bevakasha – please be quiet.

Shomrim – a community watch group in some Jewish communities.

siddur – prayerbook.

siddurim – prayerbooks.

shul – synagogue, a place of prayer.

talleisim – a garment worn while praying.

tichel – a headscarf worn by some married (and once-married) Jewish women.

tefillah – prayer.

tzitzis – a four-cornered stringed garment worn beneath the clothes, usually by boys and men.

zeeskeit – sweetheart in Yiddish.

ACKNOWLEDGMENTS

This book wouldn't have been possible without the tireless efforts of many people, each who provided something invaluable to the book, the story, or the writing process. My eternal gratitude to everyone who has made my words into this beautiful book: Meghan McCullough, Madelyn McZeal, Irene Vasquez, Johanie Martinez-Cools, Mandi Andrejka, Antonio Gonzalez Cerna, Alex Hernandez, and the whole team at Levine Querido—and, most of all, my editor, Arthur Levine, whose unfailing enthusiasm for this story shone through in every suggestion and email. I'd also like to thank Rebecca Levitan for her careful reading of the book.

I never believed the authors who said that they'd gotten their dream agent until I got mine. Tamar Rydzinski has been my rock since the start of this process, and I'm so grateful to her for putting in ceaseless energy to find the perfect fit for Aviva. I couldn't ask for a better partner in this!

I have to thank Maia, Batsheva, Zohra, Luisa, Etti, Bracha, Aimee, Sharon, and so many more of my favorite supportive nerds. And my family, who has approached my writing with a lot of cautious enthusiasm—the caution was earned, but so was the enthusiasm, I guess! Specifically, I've got to thank Ema, Tova, Ma, and Pa for being my biggest fans, and Abba, for patiently answering every ridiculously specific question I had. See? There was a point!

I wrote this book in twelve days in a rush of inspiration, and none of that would have been possible without Moshe Meir right there, extremely bemused but happy to talk me through bits of it and let me lock myself in rooms to get writing done. You definitely didn't sign up for eleven years of this, but you've never once objected and I'm so grateful for you. And shout out to Yishai, Ayala, Akiva, and Zahava for tolerating my eccentricities even when it means I'm not catering to your every whim! I promise I'll write something someday that doesn't bore you (Yishai) and that maybe one day you'll consider me a real author (Ayala). You're the best bunch of weirdos I know.

Some Notes on This Book's Production

The art for the jacket was rendered with Grumbacher oil paints
and Arteza Acrylics, on Arches 400lb Cold Pressed Watercolor
Paper by Neil Waldman. It was painted in many layers, one
on top of the next, completed with fifteen layers of sequential
color (dark to light).

The text was set in Centaur designed by Bruce Rogers in 1914.
It is a recreation of the roman type cut by fifteenth century
French engraver Nicolas Jensen. The display type, Arendahl, was
designed by Jeremy Dooley of insigne. It was composed by
Westchester Publishing Services in Danbury, CT. The book was
printed on 98gsm Yunshidai Ivory woodfree FSC™-certified
paper and bound in China.

Production was supervised by Leslie Cohen and Freesia Blizard
Jacket design by Jennifer Browne
Interior design by Semadar Megged
Edited by Arthur A. Levine

LQ

LEVINE QUERIDO

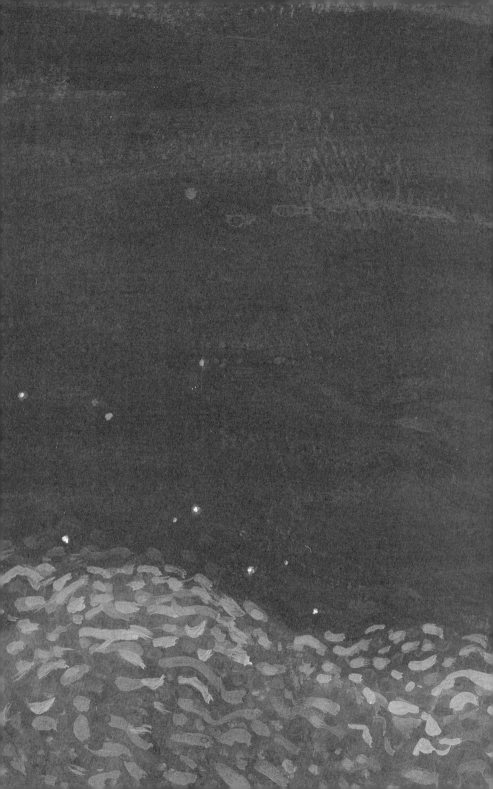